P9-ELV-244

Pixie Leaps into Trouble . . . Again!

Megan had just enough time to grab mane before Pixie rocked back on her haunches and sailed over the stone wall! . . . She landed on the other side and stopped abruptly. Megan sat panting on Pixie's back. She could hardly believe she was still on her pony. . . . Suddenly she realized where she was. She gasped and shuddered, feeling a chill run through her. She and Pixie had just jumped into *a graveyard!*

But how was she going to get out? . . . Strangely, there was no gate in the wall. . . . She didn't like the idea, but the only way out that she could see was to jump back over. . . . But there wasn't a good approach to any of the lower sections . . . everywhere she looked, gravestones blocked her path. She could get off and climb over the wall but how could she leave her pony? She didn't know what to do. Then she heard a noise that made her skin turn to ice. . . . An eery wailing sound . . .

Books in the SHORT STIRRUP CLUB™ series (by Allison Estes)

#1 Blue Ribbon Friends
#2 Ghost of Thistle Ridge

Available from MINSTREL BOOKS

Ghost of Thistle Ridge

Allison Estes

Published by POCKET BOOKS
New York   London   Toronto   Sydney   Tokyo   Singapore

This book is a work of fiction. Names, characters, places and incidents are products of the author's imagination or are used fictitiously. Any resemblance to actual events or locales or persons, living or dead, is entirely coincidental.

A MINSTREL PAPERBACK *Original*

A Minstrel Book Published by
POCKET BOOKS, a division of Simon & Schuster Inc.
1230 Avenue of the Americas, New York, NY 10020

Copyright © 1996 by Allison Estes

All rights reserved, including the right to reproduce this book or portions thereof in any form whatsoever. For information address Pocket Books, 1230 Avenue of the Americas, New York, NY 10020

ISBN: 0-671-54517-5

First Minstrel Books printing June 1996

10 9 8 7 6 5 4 3 2 1

Short Stirrup Club is a trademark of Simon & Schuster Inc.

A MINSTREL BOOK and colophon are registered trademarks of Simon & Schuster Inc.

Cover photo by Pat Hill; shot on location at Overpeck Riding Academy, New Jersey

Printed in the U.S.A.

For "Miss Laura," who taught me to post, and gave me so much more.

"Short Stirrup" is a division in horse shows, open to riders age twelve and under. Additional requirements may vary from show to show.

Ghost of
Thistle Ridge

1

MEGAN MORRISON SAT ON HER PONY UNDER THE SHADE of a giant old sycamore tree on a breezy hilltop in the back pasture of Thistle Ridge Farm. She had kicked her feet out of the stirrups and was swinging her feet in time as she counted out loud: ". . . forty-seven, forty-eight, forty-nine—fifty! Ready or not, here I come!" She opened her eyes and blinked for a moment, trying to get used to the bright sunlight.

Megan was playing a game of horseback hide-and-seek with her twin brother, Max, and their best friends, Keith Hill and Chloe Goodman. Everyone had to ride off and hide somewhere in the pasture or the woods. When the person who was "it" discovered someone's hiding place, they had to race back to the shade of the sycamore tree, which was "base." Whoever came in last had to be "it." This was the first time Megan had been "it" all week; her pony, Pixie, was so fast, she usually beat everyone back to the base.

Megan pressed her legs into Pixie's dapple-gray sides. The pony moved willingly out of the shade and into the mid-July heat. Shading her eyes, Megan scanned the rolling hills around her for signs of her brother or her friends. She couldn't see them anywhere. "Okay, Pixie," she said to the little mare, "let's go find those guys." She loosened the reins and let Pixie have her head, hoping the pony would smell the other horses and lead her to them. As they made their way down the hill, Megan remembered the day a little more than a month ago when she had first seen Thistle Ridge Farm.

The Morrisons had moved to Hickoryville from Connecticut, where eleven-year-old Megan and Max had lived all their lives. Hickoryville was a little town outside Memphis, Tennessee. The twins' mother, Dr. Rose Morrison, had been hired to head the orthopedics unit at the new medical center in Memphis. James Morrison, their father, was a very successful artist. Some of his portraits were hanging in the White House.

At first, Megan had loved the idea of moving to a new town. She thought the whole thing would be a great adventure, and that she'd find plenty of kids to be friends with at the barn where the Morrisons boarded their horses. Her brother, Max, had felt just the opposite. Megan remembered how hard it had been for him to accept the move, and how

2

she'd tried to convince him that they'd have lots of fun once they got to Thistle Ridge. But things didn't turn out quite the way she'd expected. Max had made friends with Keith right away, while Megan's first week at Thistle Ridge had been one giant disaster! In less than two days, she'd managed to insult one of the boarders, let Pixie bolt for the barn, and embarrass herself in front of the one person she'd most wanted to impress. But just when she'd begun to think she would never be happy again, she met Chloe, and the two of them had become great friends.

Megan was nearly across the flat stretch of bottom land now. The grass was already higher than Pixie's knees. Heat waves shimmered all around them. Megan looked up at the deep blue sky for a moment, just enjoying the feeling of being carried on horseback. Over in the southeast, billowy mounds of gray and white cumulus clouds were piling up. Megan wondered if the farm might get an afternoon shower. She wiped her forehead with her shirttail. Then she put a hand on Pixie's neck to see if she was getting hot. The pony's smooth coat felt sleek and dry.

Pixie started up the hill on the other side of the bottom, her feet cutting through the grass with a swishing sound. Grasshoppers buzzed off in every direction away from the pony's feet. Megan could hear the sleepy drone of cicadas buzzing in the distance. As they came to the crest of the hill, a cool breeze swept across the hilltop, flattening the grass

3

in its path. A lock of Megan's curly brown hair slipped out from under her safety helmet and blew across her eyes. She tucked it behind her ear and pulled Pixie to a halt. Then she dropped her stirrups and sat for a moment, enjoying the breeze and the view.

Megan shielded her eyes with one hand and slowly scanned the bushes at the edge of the woods just beyond the crest of the hill. She couldn't see the other kids. But she could see the big main barn, with its gleaming white-fenced paddocks in front. And she could just make out part of the main ring. Someone was riding; Megan guessed it was Sharon Wyndham. The Wyndhams owned Thistle Ridge Farm. Sharon was a member of the United States Equestrian Team and had competed in the last Olympic Games riding her big Dutch warm-blood horses, Quasar and Cuckabur. She was training for the next Olympics right now. Megan thought Sharon was the best rider she had ever seen. When Sharon wasn't riding one of her own horses, she was training someone else's, or teaching a lesson, or checking on an injured horse. At a big barn, there is always work to do; Megan had never seen Sharon stop to rest.

Sharon's husband, Jake, helped run the farm. He kept the hay mowed and the fences repaired. He also served as the announcer at the horse shows at Thistle Ridge. Jake was friendly and gentle with horses and children. Megan and Max had liked him immediately.

4

Suddenly, Megan felt Pixie start. The little mare's head went up. Her ears were pricked forward alertly. Megan quickly scooped up the reins and stuck her feet back in the stirrups. Then she looked around for whatever it was that had startled her pony.

Pixie was staring at a sprawling mound of blackberry brambles just a few yards away. Megan could feel the pony's body quivering under her calves. Then she saw what had disturbed Pixie. A deer walked calmly out from behind the bushes and stood staring at Megan and Pixie.

Megan held her breath. There were deer all over the one hundred seventy acres owned by the Wyndhams. The first time Pixie had encountered them, however, she had reacted by bolting for the barn. Megan felt her own heart begin to beat very quickly and felt a nervous quake in the pit of her stomach. She shortened the reins and held them firmly. She was prepared to deal with Pixie if she bolted, but she hoped she wouldn't have to. The last time Pixie had bolted with her, she'd ended up jumping a four-foot fence surrounding one of the paddocks. Megan had stayed on, but she wasn't looking forward to doing that again for quite some time. She shortened the reins another inch and gave Pixie a nudge with her right leg, moving her hindquarters to the left so they'd be facing the deer. Then she waited nervously.

Pixie gave a big snort and stared at the deer, who continued to stare back at them. Then, to Megan's

5

surprise, she saw another shape come out of the blackberry brambles. It was a little baby fawn!

"Oooh," Megan said softly. "You are beautiful!" The fawn came and stood by its mother, who licked at her baby's ear and looked proudly back at Megan and Pixie. She seemed to be showing off her baby.

Pixie snorted again and then put her head down and took a step toward the deer. Megan patted her neck. "Good girl," she said encouragingly, glad to see that Pixie wasn't panicking.

Then the doe turned and walked back behind the bushes. The fawn followed. To Megan's surprise, Pixie followed, too! Megan started to pull up but then decided to let her go after them; maybe it would help her get used to deer.

The doe led them down a little dip and into the woods. They came out in a clearing surrounded on three sides by trees. The fourth side sloped down toward a weathered, wooden fence that separated the Wyndhams' land from the neighboring farm. Not a telephone pole or a building was in sight. Megan was thinking that this land must have looked just the same for a hundred years.

The doe walked to the far side of the clearing and stood near a little pile of stones. Pixie's curiosity about the deer seemed to be getting the better of her fear. She moved slowly closer, until they were only a few feet away. The fawn took a step toward them and stood sniffing the air with its dainty nose. Its little body was as red as a fox's and still covered with white spots. Megan had never come so close to a wild animal before. She wanted to reach out and pet its soft coat, but instead she sat very still and watched the two deer, amazed at their boldness. She had forgotten all about the game of hide-and-seek.

The doe moved closer to the pile of stones. With a slender leg, she pawed at them. One stone turned over and rolled off the pile. The doe put her head down and sniffed at it, then backed away as if she were somehow satisfied. She looked around for her baby.

The fawn had been watching Pixie contentedly. Now it gave a joyful little leap into the air and began to race around them, bucking and playing. Pixie snorted again loudly, then whinnied, startling the fawn in mid-leap. It landed on shaky legs and stood staring at Megan and Pixie, then just as quickly jumped away and began to play again. Before she could help it, Megan laughed out loud. The doe froze and stared at her, as if she had just noticed that a human was near. Then she turned and bounded off with her baby, vanishing into the woods with a flash of white tail.

"Oh, Pixie, weren't they beautiful?" Megan sighed with delight. "I wish I hadn't laughed and scared them." She looked at the pile of stones where the doe had stood moments before. Suddenly, she saw a flash of sunlight glinting off something shiny near the bottom of the pile.

Megan slid off of Pixie and took the reins over the pony's head. She squatted down near where

7

she'd seen the flash of light and began searching through the grass. Then she saw it again. In the hole left by the stone the deer had turned over was an oval-shaped object about the size of a large walnut. Megan tried to pick it up, but it was attached to something stuck in the ground. She dug around it and pulled up a chain, tarnished and embedded with dirt.

She was just about to try cleaning it off when she heard someone speaking. The sound came from the trees behind her. She recognized Keith's voice and realized he must be hiding in the woods nearby. Megan had forgotten all about the game of hide-and-seek. She stuck the chain into her shirt pocket, mounted up, and turned Pixie toward the woods. Before they had trotted twenty feet, she spied Max on his horse, Popsicle, hiding behind the tangled roots of a fallen tree.

"I see you, Max, behind that old tree!" When she saw him come trotting out of the woods, she cantered away toward the "base." She had to slow Pixie going down the hill. By the time she got to the bottom, Max was right behind her. She looked over her shoulder, and they grinned at each other, anticipating the fun that was about to begin. Then they were off, galloping across the bottom.

Megan heard the thudding of hooves and the slicing sound as the horses' legs swiped through the grass. Grasshoppers buzzed angrily away. They were heading up the next hill now. Megan bent forward into a two-point or "jumping" position so her

8

weight would shift off Pixie's back. She grabbed a handful of Pixie's mane as she felt the little mare's powerful hindquarters dig into the hillside, propelling them toward the top. As she reached the crest of the hill, she glanced back and saw she was ahead of Max by several feet.

At the top of the hill, she saw the tree that was "base." She glanced back once more and saw Max and Popsicle come over the crest of the hill right behind her. Then she closed her legs against Pixie's sides and clucked, urging the pony forward.

Pixie didn't need much urging. She doubled her strides and galloped for the tree, leaving Max and Popsicle behind. Megan felt the wind rushing past her face. She was laughing as she made it to the shade and pulled up, panting. She gave Pixie a big pat on her dappled neck. Max and Popsicle came up a moment later.

"What happened, little brother?" Megan kidded him. She was older than Max by twenty minutes and never tired of reminding him of that. "Can't you make that horse of yours go any faster?"

Max shook his head. He was laughing, too. "I don't know how you make that pony's little legs go like that, but she just flies!"

"That's why I love ponies; they can do everything horses do, but they do it quicker!" Megan said. "I hope I don't get much taller. Then I can keep riding ponies for the rest of my life."

"You're going to look pretty funny doing the big

jumpers at the National Horse Show on a pony," Max joked.

"Forget the National Horse Show," Megan said. "I'm going to the Olympics!"

"You'd better get your elbows in then, shorty," Max told her. "You were galloping for the tree with your arms flapping like chicken wings!" Max flapped his own elbows in a birdlike imitation of his sister. Though they were twins, the two looked nothing alike. Max was a few inches taller than his sister, who had inherited her father's looks and build. Max had his mother's light hair and blue-gray eyes.

Popsicle gave a whinny, which was answered by Keith's horse, Penny. Megan looked up and saw Keith and Penny trotting toward them, with Chloe close behind on Bo Peep. Popsicle and Penny looked almost exactly alike. They were both chestnut quarter horses with four white stockings on their legs and white "bald" faces. It would have been hard to tell them apart, except that Popsicle had two blue eyes, while Penny had one brown and one blue.

"That was some race!" Keith said when he reached the tree. He had shiny black hair that he kept pulled back in a ponytail. His face and arms were very tan. Keith's father was Mexican, and his mother was Native American. "I was hiding right next to Max," Keith said to Megan. "I thought for sure you'd see me first."

"Pixie is so fast!" Chloe exclaimed. "It's just

amazing." She leaned over Bo Peep's wide neck and gave the pony a hug. "Peeps could never keep up with her." Bo Peep was a sleek, black Exmoor pony, with the fattest neck Megan had ever seen. Her neck was almost as broad as her belly, which was also a generous size. Everyone at the barn affectionately called Bo Peep's neck "the airbag." Bo Peep was a school horse, which meant that she belonged to the stable and was used for lessons. But Chloe got along with her so well that Sharon Wyndham let her ride her pretty much whenever she wanted. Chloe's own pony was recovering from an injury that might take most of the summer to heal.

"Let's play one more time before we go in," Keith suggested.

"Max, you're it," Megan said.

"I know, I know. What's that?" he asked, pointing at Megan's shirt.

"What?"

"There's something sticking out of your pocket."

"Oh! I almost forgot. When Pixie and I were looking for you guys, we saw some deer—"

"Uh-oh," Max said. He and Keith had been with Megan the time Pixie spooked at the deer and bolted for the barn. "Was Pixie okay?"

"She was fine," Megan said impatiently. "But listen! It was a mother deer and a little baby fawn. Pixie followed them—"

"She *followed* them?" Max sounded incredulous.

"Yes! Into the woods. And they led us to sort of

a clear place over on the back hill. The mother deer went to a pile of rocks and pawed at them. When the deer finally ran away, I found this." Megan held up the chain.

"What is it?" Keith asked curiously.

"Let me see it," Max said in a no-nonsense tone of voice.

Megan handed it over to him. He examined it. "It's a locket. See? I think it opens here." He dug a fingernail in the seam at the edge and tried to pull it open. "It's really jammed, probably from all the dirt." Max untucked his shirt and began rubbing the front of the locket. "There's something on it here, like an engraving." He squinted at it, trying to make out the markings.

"Let me see it," Megan said, reaching for it.

Max handed her the locket. She rubbed it briskly against her shirt, then studied the engraving. "It's initials, I think," she said. "But it's that fancy swirly lettering that's so hard to read. It looks like M. K. . . . something. I can't make out the last letter. And it's got a stone set into the center. Do you think it could be a diamond?"

"Who knows?" Max shrugged.

"Who cares?" Keith added. "C'mon, let's play."

"I don't think we can," Chloe said. Her green eyes were serious. "Look at the sky." She pointed past the trees toward the southeast. The clouds that Megan had seen gathering earlier were piled up into a mountain of gray thunderheads that boiled up at the top. A gust of wind carried with it a few stray leaves and the smell of rain.

"It's coming this way," Chloe said anxiously. Lightning flashed in the belly of the clouds. A few seconds later, they heard the rumble of thunder.

"We shouldn't be out here in this," Max said.

"No kidding!" Megan said. She already had to raise her voice to be heard above the wind, which was stirring the tree overhead. Lightning flashed again, followed by a rumble of thunder.

"Let's go!" Keith yelled.

The three of them followed him down the hill and trotted toward the barn. They were halfway there when the first splatter of raindrops hit. Megan glanced behind her and saw that the storm clouds were almost over them. A brilliant bolt of lightning cracked loudly, followed by a deafening boom of thunder. Pixie broke into a canter.

"Come on, you guys!" Megan yelled, slowing Pixie. She patted her shirt pocket to make sure the locket was safe. Then she trotted with the others toward the barn as the rain started to come down.

2

THE CHILDREN MADE THEIR WAY UP AND DOWN THE hills and through the woods as fast as they dared. The horses knew they were headed for home, so it was tricky trying to hurry back and still keep them in control. Megan especially had her hands full with Pixie, who was the most excitable of the four horses.

The wind seemed to come from every direction at once. As they came through the last section of trees before the barn, Megan looked back in time to see lightning strike a big pine tree, just inches away from Bo Peep! She gasped as the tree tore into halves, as if it had been split with a giant, invisible ax.

Bo Peep, who was usually content bringing up the rear, gave a frightened snort and charged past the others, galloping the last stretch up the hill.

Chloe was pulling on the reins with all her might, but the pony would not slow down. It was all Megan could do to keep Pixie from running after her. She knew it was dangerous to run toward a barn—a horse might get into the habit of it and end up running every time he was turned toward home. She gave two firm tugs on the reins to get Pixie's attention and was relieved that she was able to keep her trotting.

The rain was coming down in torrents by the time they reached the barn. Megan, Max, and Keith dismounted and led the horses into the welcome shelter of the stables. There they all stood, dripping and panting in the peaceful barn, while the storm went on outside. Chloe patted the terrified Bo Peep, whose eyes still showed white around them.

"Whew," Megan said, wringing out her shirt. "That was close!"

"Too close!" Max agreed.

"Did you see the lightning strike that tree?" Megan said. "We rode right underneath it a second before it got hit!"

"I thought that tree was going to fall right on top of me," Chloe said shakily, pulling off her helmet. Her pale blond hair stuck to her wet face. "I didn't know Bo Peep could go that fast! I guess she thought it was going to fall on top of her, too."

"Haven't y'all got sense enough to come in outta the rain?" A tall, friendly-looking girl stood in the aisle. She wore cutoff shorts and a T-shirt that was so dirty from working around horses, it was impos-

15

sible to tell what color it had once been. She stuck her fists into her hips and looked at all of them. "Well?" she said.

"Allie, the storm came up so fast! None of us even noticed until it was almost on top of us," Keith said.

"Next time, keep an eye on the weather," Allie said. Allie was the best groom at Thistle Ridge. She knew every inch of every horse in the whole barn. She began checking the horses and ponies to see if they were too hot to be put away. "You know how a storm can come up fast over these hills this time of year. Land sakes! Chloe, what happened to this pony? I've never seen her afraid of anything."

They told Allie about the lightning striking the tree just as they passed by it. She went and looked out the back door to see the damage. The mangled tree was split in two, with a big, charred, black streak up its middle.

"Well, y'all were lucky, that's all!" Allie shook her head in disbelief. "That was just too close. I reckon somebody was looking out for you."

With Allie's help, the children untacked the horses and ponies, rubbed them down with towels to dry them, and put them away. Max had an extra towel in his tack trunk that they used to dry themselves off as best they could. Then the saddles and bridles had to be cleaned with saddle soap, wiped down and hung up to dry, and the bits rinsed clean with warm water.

"Boy, am I thirsty," Megan exclaimed when they had finished.

"Let's go get sodas," Keith said.

The barn formed a T shape, with the main aisle at the top of the T. Outside the second, shorter aisle was a patio with a picnic table, an old brick barbecue grill, and, just under the eaves, a soda machine. The storm had nearly passed, leaving everything cool and dripping. The kids usually sat on the picnic table, but it was wet, so they went back into the barn.

Max and Keith sat on Max's tack trunk outside Popsicle's stall. Megan and Chloe sat across from them on Megan's trunk. They drank their sodas and chatted about the day. Megan gulped down the last of her soda and bent down to set the empty can on the barn floor.

"Megan, something fell out of your pocket," Chloe said.

"Oh, the locket." Megan picked it up and hopped back up on the trunk. "I almost forgot about it."

The rain had loosened much of the dirt stuck in the chain. Megan rubbed at the locket with her shirttail as she told the group again how the deer had led her and Pixie to the pile of stones. "It was almost as if the mother deer wanted me to find this," Megan said, holding up the necklace to inspect it. Much of the grime and tarnish had come off, revealing a very elegant silver locket. The stone set above the initials sparkled brilliantly in the late-afternoon light.

17

"Isn't it pretty?" Chloe exclaimed. "Can I see it, Megan?"

Megan passed it to Chloe. "I wonder where it came from," Chloe said, trying to open the locket. "Boy, it's really stuck." She pulled a little harder on it, and suddenly the locket sprang open. "Look!" She handed it back to Megan.

Inside the locket were a little brass key and two tiny, faded pictures—one of a woman's face and the other the head of a white horse. "Neat!" Megan crowed. "I wonder what the key goes to."

"I wonder if someone was riding back there and lost it," Keith said.

"Maybe you should turn it in to the lost-and-found," Max suggested.

Megan's face fell. "I guess you're right. Shoot. I wanted to keep it."

"Well, maybe if no one claims it after a while, you can have it," Chloe said.

"Have what?" Jake Wyndham came strolling down the aisle toward them. He wore very broken-in jeans with a plain T-shirt, cowboy boots, and an Atlanta Braves baseball cap. He stood with his thumbs hooked into the pockets of his jeans and waited for them to answer.

"Hey, Jake!" Keith was always glad to see Jake. The two of them were close, partly because they were the only two people who rode Western at Thistle Ridge. Everyone else rode English. "Jake, take a look at this." Keith pointed to the locket.

Megan handed it over to Jake, who examined it

closely. "Where did you find this, Megan?" Jake asked her. He listened intently while Megan explained again how she'd followed the deer. When she told how she'd been able to get so close to them, he shook his head in wonder.

"So what do you think, Jake?" Megan finished. "Do you know anyone who might have lost it?"

"This is old," Jake told her. "And I believe that's a real diamond set into it. Offhand, I can't think of anybody with those initials, but I reckon Max is right; it's valuable, so we ought to at least put up a notice that it's been found. I tell you what—let me show it to Sharon and see if she recognizes it. Then we'll put up a notice about it. If no one claims it in a week, it's yours."

"Okay," Megan said to Jake. To Chloe she whispered, "But I hope no one does!"

The next day was Monday, the opening of summer riding day camp at Thistle Ridge Farm. The campers were divided into three groups, according to their ages. There were quite a lot of little kids and ten or twelve older kids. Keith's big sister, Haley, was in the older group. The middle group was quite small—Megan and Max and Keith, who was ten, and Chloe, who was twelve but little for her age. Chloe's instructor, Leigh, had been assigned to their group.

"Is this it?" Megan asked Leigh. "There aren't any more kids in our group?"

"I guess not," Leigh said.

"Good!" Chloe said, hugging Leigh. "Now we can have you all to ourselves."

"The Short Stirrup Club rides again!" Megan said happily.

"So let's get started," Leigh said. "I'm lucky—you all can get your own horses ready. Meet me outside the back door in twenty minutes. I'm taking you out on a trail ride."

"All right!" Max and Keith high-fived each other. The boys always jumped at a chance to ride all over the one hundred seventy acres of hills and woods and pastures that made up Thistle Ridge Farm.

Megan didn't care whether she rode in the ring or in the pasture. She was happy to be on her pony whatever she was doing. She led Pixie out of her stall, clipped the cross-ties to her halter, and began to groom her, loving the feel of her silky coat after she brushed her clean. Pixie nosed at her pocket hopefully. Megan dug under her chaps and pulled a roll of breath mints out of her pocket. She gave one to Pixie, who crunched it happily.

When Megan finished tacking up Pixie, she led her down the aisle and out the back door. Keith and Max were already mounted up and waiting.

Leigh came around the side of the barn leading Hot Shot, one of the school horses. He was an old Tennessee walking horse who was so smart he could tell right away if his riders were experienced—and if they weren't, they wouldn't be on him for long! He was ridden mostly by advanced riders in lessons or by instructors on trail rides. All the instructors loved him and had nicknamed him "the Cadillac" because his gaits were so smooth and comfortable.

While Megan was tightening Pixie's girth, Chloe came out of the barn leading Bo Peep. Keith and Max exchanged exasperated looks.

"Why are girls always the last to get ready?" Max sighed impatiently.

"Yeah, we've been waiting forever. Can't you hurry it up?" Keith complained.

"I'm not getting on unless I know my girth is tight," Megan said, giving it a final tug.

"Did you tighten your girth, Keith?" Leigh asked.

"It's not a girth, it's a cinch," Keith told her. "On a Western saddle, you tighten the cinch."

Leigh frowned at him. "Did you tighten the *cinch?*"

He shrugged and replied, "I got it as tight as I could."

Penny, Keith's quarter horse mare, was notorious for puffing up her belly with a deep breath as the cinch was tightened. If Keith didn't check it again before he rode off, the saddle could end up slipping to the side. Keith had been dumped off more than once when the saddle slipped, but he never seemed to learn.

At last, Chloe and Megan were mounted up.

"Ready?" Leigh asked.

"Ready!" everyone shouted.

"Let's go!"

They had just started down the hill when there was a shout from behind them. Leigh turned Hot Shot around to see who was calling them. A woman in white breeches, tall black boots, and a lavender riding shirt with a monogrammed collar was standing in the doorway of the barn, waving at them.

"Yoo-hoo! Leigh!" she called. "Leigh, come back here. Amanda is coming with you!"

A girl about Megan's height stood next to the woman. She was impeccably dressed in expensive jodhpurs and a smaller version of her mother's monogrammed shirt. Her paddock boots were so shiny they hardly looked worn, and her blond hair was perfectly braided and tied with satin ribbons that matched the pastel purple of her shirt.

"Who is that?" Chloe said, squinting into the bright morning sun.

"It's Amanda Sloane," Megan said, feeling her happy mood sink down toward her heels.

"Oh," Chloe said, sounding equally disappointed.

Amanda Sloane was eleven, the same age as Max and Megan, but she wasn't very friendly to them or the other kids, unless she wanted something from them. She was an only child whose parents were very wealthy. Amanda was the sort of person who never seemed to understand what it meant to work for something. She was used to having everything she wanted bought for her.

"Now then, Amandasue, I have told them they

must wait for you. You go get your horse," Mrs. Sloane directed.

"Hurry up, please, Amanda," Leigh called. "We're running late already. Bo Peep has a lesson with the little kids after this, and she has to jump later in the afternoon. I want to be back in time to give her a rest between classes."

"Oh, poor Peeps." Chloe patted the shiny black mound of muscle that was Bo Peep's neck. "She has to work so hard during camp."

"If that pony worked any less, she'd be too wide to fit through her stall door," Leigh observed, shaking her head in amusement. "Look at the size of her belly." She glanced at her watch and sighed. "It's just like the Sloanes to bring Amanda late and then expect everyone to wait for them."

"Here we go again," Max groaned. "Waiting for the girls."

"What are you complaining for? I thought Amanda was your girlfriend," Keith teased.

"No way!" Max protested.

"I think she likes you," Keith insisted.

"Keith's right," Megan joined in. "Aren't you supposed to have dinner at her house soon?" The first time Amanda had met Max, she had invited him over to her house for dinner.

"Be quiet, Megan," Max growled.

"Didn't they name their dog after you or something like that?" Megan persisted. Max's face was turning red with embarrassment. He was usually unfazed by teasing, so Megan was enjoying watching her brother squirm. She went on, imitating Amanda's Southern drawl: "Oh, we have a *juuhman shehpahd* named Max! Isn't that funny?"

Keith and Chloe broke into giggles, and even Leigh had to smile. Megan's imitation of Amanda was perfect, right down to the tilt of her head and the fake smile. Max pretended to be busy adjusting a stirrup.

"By the way, Chloe, how's Jump for Joy?" Leigh asked.

"Well, he's still on stall rest. So far, there's not much change in his leg, but Dr. Pepper says he doesn't expect to see it get better for a while. I've been cold-hosing it every day, as many times as I can."

Leigh nodded. Jump for Joy had been Amanda Sloane's fancy show pony. He had cost Amanda's father twenty thousand dollars, but the pony had pulled a ligament when he slipped in the mud at the last Thistle Ridge horse show. When Pepper Jordan, the veterinarian, told Amanda's father the pony would need months to recover, Mr. Sloane had ordered that the pony be put down.

Everyone had been horrified that the Sloanes would actually have Jump for Joy put down rather than spend the money to pay his board and vet bills while he recovered. "Dr. Pepper," as the kids called Pepper Jordan, had said the pony probably would make a good recovery, given enough time and the proper treatment. But he might never jump again.

Chloe, who'd been saving every dollar she earned

from baby-sitting and doing chores so that she could buy a pony, had been heartbroken. She had always loved Jump for Joy. She used to do barn chores for Amanda just to be allowed to groom him.

It had been Megan's idea to give the pony to Chloe instead of putting him down. Sharon Wyndham had persuaded Mr. Sloane to sign Jump for Joy's papers over to Chloe. Now she was taking care of the pony and working off his board, since her mom couldn't afford to pay for it. Chloe's parents were divorced. She lived with her mom and her little brother, Michael.

"Amanda! Watch out!"

They all looked up to see Mrs. Sloane being practically dragged out of the barn by Amanda's new horse, Prince Charming. Prince was all white like Jump for Joy, but there the similarity ended.

He was a great big "appendix" quarter horse, which is a quarter horse crossed with a thoroughbred. Quarter horses are known for being good-natured, versatile, and intelligent. Thoroughbreds are fast and stubborn. Prince Charming had inherited the powerful hindquarters of his quarter horse dam and the stubborn temperament of his thoroughbred sire. He would have been a handful for any rider, but when Amanda was on him, there might as well have been no one on his back.

Amanda was not a very capable rider, though she had done well in horse shows on Jump for Joy. He was the very special sort of pony who did it all for the rider, calmly and willingly jumping anything he was pointed at. Prince Charming, however, was not so special. Sharon Wyndham had tried to convince the Sloanes that Prince was too much horse for Amanda to handle, but they hadn't listened. They had only been impressed by the horse's grand, arching white neck and his ability to jump big jumps.

Megan thought Prince Charming was beautiful. She longed to ride him herself, and she was hoping that she could talk Amanda into letting her get on him. Megan watched with amusement as Mrs. Sloane hung on to one of Prince's reins and tried to lead him out the door while Amanda cowered nearby.

Leigh rolled her eyes. "Stay here," she said to the kids. She trotted Hot Shot up to the barn and dismounted. Holding Hot Shot's reins in one hand, she took Prince's reins in the other and, with a growl and a cluck, got him out the door. "Come here, Amanda, and I'll give you a leg up."

Amanda fastened her safety helmet under her chin and slowly walked over to Prince's left side. Leigh took Amanda's left leg and boosted her up to the saddle. Grabbing the reins under Prince's chin to steady him as he danced around, she held on until Amanda had her feet in the stirrups. Then Leigh mounted up on Hot Shot again and turned toward the path that led down the hill and into the pasture. "Let's go!" she called to the kids.

3

LEIGH LED THE FIVE RIDERS DOWN THE HILL BEHIND THE barn, following the trail that led through a stand of trees, past the back paddock and into the pastures of Thistle Ridge Farm. Amanda was having trouble keeping Prince Charming away from the other horses. He was a nosy, doggy sort of horse. He trotted right up to Bo Peep's round hindquarters, and the pony kicked out in annoyance at him.

"Leigh!" Amanda called out. "Chloe's horse just tried to kick Prince Charming."

"But you rode right up her tail," Chloe protested. "You're not supposed to be so close. You're supposed to keep a horse length between you and any other horses."

"I am a perfectly safe distance from that pony. She just has a mean disposition. Even my mother said so. Bo Peep kicked at my horse for no reason, no reason at all," Amanda insisted, as Prince began creeping up on Pixie.

"Everyone please try and stay in a space by yourself," Leigh admonished. "You all know the rule: one horse length from any other horse in any direction."

"Except for Penny and Popsicle," Max added.

"Yeah, we'd cause more problems if we tried to separate these two," Keith said with a laugh. Penny and Popsicle really were nearly inseparable when they were out together. If there was such a thing as love at first sight between two horses, it had happened to them. They were walking so close that they were exactly in stride with each other. From time to time, Max's and Keith's feet would bump each other because they were so close.

"I still think they're related," Max said. "They must remember each other from when they were babies."

"Okay, but everybody else, keep your distance!" Leigh said. "Chloe, watch out for your pony's hindquarters. You know she kicks; be responsible."

Megan shot Amanda a look that said she knew who had caused the problem. Then she circled Pixie around and came up beside Bo Peep, being careful not to get too close. She knew that even the gentlest horse will sometimes kick, and that mares are more likely to react to other horses being too near.

"I know that wasn't your fault, Chloe," Megan said in a hushed tone. "Everyone knows Amanda can't control that horse."

"I can't believe she would ride right up on Peeps

like that," Chloe said. "Everyone knows she kicks out."

"Amanda's just jealous because you ended up with her pony," Megan told her.

They watched as Amanda began to ride closer and closer up behind Penny and Popsicle. Megan shook her head in disgust. Besides being such a snob, Amanda was downright dangerous to be riding with.

On their way through the woods, they passed the tree that had been struck by lightning. They stopped and stared wordlessly at the wreck of the big tree. Chloe patted Bo Peep nervously.

"Wow," Leigh said. "This is the tree you were telling me about?"

"Yeah," Chloe said with a gulp.

"Boy, were you lucky. If it did that to the tree, imagine what it would have done to a human, or a horse," Leigh exclaimed.

"We were almost barbecue," Chloe said.

"You mean 'Bo'-becue," Megan joked. They all laughed.

Soon, Leigh had them trotting along a fence line at the base of one of the hills. Blackberry and honeysuckle grew over the old cedar rails. In some places, the fence had rotted and fallen down long ago, but the vines and brambles were so thick, no animal could have passed through them even without a fence.

"Ouch! Oh, my arm! Oh! Y'all, *help!*"

Leigh made Hot Shot walk and turned around to see what the trouble was. It was Amanda who had called out. She'd let Prince Charming trot right up on Penny. Then she'd turn aside at the last second to avoid actually bumping into the other horse. She had run right into a large blackberry bramble. The thorns had snagged her clothes, and even one of her perfect blond braids was now hopelessly entangled in the briars.

Prince, of course, was making the situation worse by prancing and jigging impatiently. Several thorny branches had caught in his mane and tail. He kept tossing his head and swishing his tail to shake them, but they only became more entangled.

Amanda was nearly hysterical by now. She had dropped the reins when her hands were scratched by the briars. It was clear that Prince Charming was just about to lose what little patience he had.

Max was the closest to Amanda. He rode up alongside Prince, put his reins in one hand, and with the other managed to lean over far enough to grab Prince's reins. He steadied the big horse, ducking a branch loaded with berries and thorns that waved dangerously close to his face.

"Megan, dismount, quickly!" Leigh said.

She did as she was told. Leigh handed her Hot Shot's reins. Megan stood and held Pixie and Hot Shot while Leigh hurried to help Max and Amanda.

Though Max was doing his best to hold him back, Prince had kept on inching forward in an attempt to escape. Amanda was leaning far back in the saddle and off to one side, unable to move because of the thorns holding her hair and clothes. Megan could see the long scratches on Amanda's arms and face beginning to bleed. Her eyes were squeezed shut, and she was whimpering in pain and fright. Megan began to feel sorry for her. It was going to hurt just as much getting out of all those stickers as it had getting into them.

"Hang on, Amanda, we'll get you unstuck," Leigh told her. But she sounded doubtful. She was trying gingerly to unclamp the briars from Amanda's clothes without getting stuck herself, which was nearly impossible.

Prince kept trying to step forward every few seconds, in spite of Max's hold on his reins.

"Keith," Leigh said finally, "ride back to the barn and see if you can find Jake. Tell him to come quick, and he'd better bring some big clippers. And hurry!"

Keith nodded and loped off toward the barn on Penny. In less than ten minutes, Megan spotted Jake driving along the fence line where they'd been riding, the old blue truck squeaking and bouncing along. Keith and Penny loped along behind. Jake pulled up and jumped out of the truck.

With a large pair of hedge clippers, Jake went to work snipping the thick branches that held Amanda. He had almost freed her when a stray branch caught her in the arm again. Amanda screamed, frightening Prince Charming, who lunged forward, yanking Max's arm.

"Let go, Max," Jake yelled. He did, and Prince Charming scooted out from under Amanda, leaving her sitting in the grass under the briars, with pieces of blackberry branches stuck all over her.

"Dad-gum," Jake observed, watching Prince Charming trot away toward the back pasture. "That animal doesn't even know the way back to the barn. We'll have a heck of a time catching him, that's for sure." Just as he said that, Prince Charming put a foot through his reins, yanking himself in the mouth. He jerked his head up in surprise, breaking the reins, then trotted off over the hill.

"Amanda, are you all right?" Jake asked her.

"Oooooh," Amanda wailed.

Leigh and Jake pulled the rest of the briars from Amanda's skin and clothes and hair while she squirmed and shrieked.

"Amanda, this'd be a whole lot easier if you kept still," Leigh observed, untangling a branch from Amanda's hair.

When they had finally pulled most of the stickers out of her, Amanda was scratched and bleeding and completely disheveled. One braid was loose, and she had a big tear in her expensive riding shirt. As Jake helped her into the cab of his truck, Amanda was still sniveling.

Jake rested one elbow on the windowsill of his truck and said to Leigh, "I'll come back and look for that horse after I take Amanda to the barn. Don't y'all worry about him. Go on and finish your trail ride."

The group of riders waved at him and watched until the truck had squeaked and jounced out of sight. "It's too bad she can't finish the trail ride," Megan said, not sounding particularly sorry.

"Too bad for Amanda," Keith said.

"I can't say I'll miss her," Max added.

"I hope Prince Charming is okay," Chloe said sincerely.

Leigh took Hot Shot's reins from Megan. "Thanks for holding him, Megan. Here, I'll give you a leg up." She boosted Megan to the saddle, then mounted up herself. "Okay, let's try this trail ride one more time. But any more trouble, and we're heading back to the barn! Everybody understand?"

"We won't cause any trouble," Megan said.

"We'll do exactly what you say," Chloe joined in.

"We promise," Keith said.

"Where are you taking us?" Max asked.

"You'll see," Leigh said mysteriously as she trotted off.

The riders soon came to a gate separating one pasture from another. Megan recognized it as the place where Pixie had spooked and bolted with her after jumping the fence. Megan had been with Max and Keith that day, but she shouldn't have been jumping without an adult. She wouldn't ever do it again, that was for sure!

"I'll get the gate, okay, Leigh?" Keith begged.

"Go ahead," Leigh said amiably.

Keith walked Penny to the gate, unhooked the chain from the nail that held it, and opened the gate without getting off his horse. When everyone had ridden through, he closed it again. Then he smiled grandly as he gave Penny a big pat on the neck. "Good girl," he told her.

"That is so cool," Max said admiringly. "I'm going to try to do that with Popsicle."

"Good job, Keith," Leigh said. "I'd have to dismount to get the gates if it weren't for you."

Megan was looking at Hot Shot with a frown. Leigh had paused to let him scratch at a fly on his right flank. He was bent nearly double, standing on three legs. He lifted his right hind and brought it forward, rubbing his teeth hard against the itchy spot.

"How does he balance on three legs like that?" Megan wondered out loud.

"He's a smart one," Leigh smiled, patting him fondly on his proud neck. When he'd finished scratching, he walked on again. Like all the other horses, he swished his tail constantly to keep the flies off his rear and sides. But suddenly, Megan noticed that Hot Shot's tail was different from a normal horse's tail. It was long and wavy and reddish-gold, but it stood up and then crooked off to the left.

"Leigh, why does Hot Shot's tail look like that?" Megan asked.

"Hot Shot's a Tennessee walking horse," Leigh explained "For many years, it was fashionable to break the tailbones of walking horses and saddle-bred horses and reset them so they stood up, the way a horse will sometimes naturally hold up his tail when he's feeling good. The people who bred them thought it made them look better. Whoever set Hot Shot's tail botched the job. That's why it's all crooked."

"You mean they actually *broke* the bone, just to make it look some way they thought it ought to look?" Max sounded incredulous. "That's terrible!"

"That's so mean!" Megan exclaimed at the same time.

"It *is* mean," Leigh agreed. "A horse's tail is an important tool in his life. They keep away the flies with their tails, and that helps keep away the diseases spread by flies. Hot Shot can only reach his left side with his tail. That's why I allow him to stop and scratch like that."

"Do they still break horses' tails?" Max asked Leigh.

"No, thank goodness."

"The poor things," Chloe said. She looked as though she might cry.

"People can be so bad to animals," Megan agreed.

"When I grow up, I'm going to work for one of those organizations that protect animals," Chloe declared.

"Good for you," Leigh said.

They had come over the crest of a low hill and were looking at a wide, shimmering lake bordered by pine trees. The wind rippled the surface of the lake invitingly. Megan felt cooler just looking at the water, and she was wishing she could somehow go in it.

"Wouldn't it be great to go swimming right now?" Megan said wistfully.

"It sure would," Max agreed.

"Let's do it," Keith said.

"Can we, Leigh?" Chloe asked. "Pleeease."

"What do you think I brought you here for?" Leigh said, chuckling. "I'm looking forward to this myself. Okay, saddles off!"

"Hurray!" Keith yelled, getting off so quickly he could have fallen off slower. He began loosening Penny's cinch.

"Come on. Megan, Max, what are you waiting for?" Chloe was pulling off Bo Peep's saddle.

"I don't understand." Megan sounded puzzled. She sat on top of Pixie and watched the others. "How are we going to go swimming? Someone would have to hold the horses. And why are you taking off the saddles?"

"So they don't get wet, silly." Chloe hastily kicked off her shoes and led Bo Peep into the lake. When it was up to her thighs, she grabbed some mane and pulled herself up onto the pony's back. Keith did the same. Still mounted, Megan and Max exchanged a bewildered glance.

Suddenly, Max understood. "Meg," he said with delight, "we're going to swim with the horses!"

4

MEGAN AND MAX DISMOUNTED AS QUICKLY AS THEY could, unsaddled their horses, and unzipped their chaps. They were both glad they were wearing shorts underneath. By the time they had their boots and helmets off, Leigh was already in the water on Hot Shot.

"Megan?" Max said very sweetly.

"Yes, Max?" Megan said suspiciously.

"How about giving me a leg up?"

Megan hastily boosted Max up on Popsicle. Then she easily hopped up on Pixie and grinned slyly at her brother. "Race you to the lake," she said, and thumped Pixie in the ribs with her bare heels.

Pixie cantered quickly toward the shore. Max was right beside her on Popsicle. Popsicle trotted right into the lake, probably because he saw Penny already standing in the water. But Pixie cantered up to the

37

edge of the water and stopped, planting her front legs firmly and ducking her head. Megan went sailing right over Pixie's head! She landed sitting in the water up to her chest, still holding the reins in one hand.

For a moment, everyone was shocked. Even Pixie looked surprised. Megan was the most surprised of all. Pixie had stopped so suddenly that she had had no time to react by sitting back.

"Megan, are you all right?" Leigh asked.

Megan started to giggle. So did Max. Then everyone broke up laughing.

"Megan, that was the most interesting dismount I ever saw," Leigh teased.

Megan stood up and took a bow, as if she'd just put on a show. "Thank you, thank you," she said. "And now, for my next trick, I will attempt to lead The Amazing Pixie into the lake!"

Everyone was still laughing. Pixie was the only one who didn't seemed amused. Megan waded over to her, giving her a pat on the neck. It took some coaxing, but the pony finally put a foot into the water and took a tentative sip, then a good long drink. Then she let Megan lead her in a little further, bit by bit, until the water touched her belly. Megan grabbed a handful of mane and pulled herself up on Pixie's back.

"Ta-daaah!" She dropped the reins and gestured grandly, palms up. Everyone applauded.

"Oh, you are such a brave pony!" Megan hugged Pixie around her neck. Then she splashed a little water on her. Pixie didn't seem to mind, now that she was all the way in.

"I guess she wanted to test the water before she jumped in," Chloe said, laughing.

"She sure got her point across," Megan said.

"You guys, look at Penny." Max pointed.

Penny really loved the water. She stood chest-deep in it, striking repeatedly with one foreleg, splashing great amounts of water in all directions. Keith was laughing hysterically and squinting to keep the water out of his eyes.

Of course Popsicle had to join in. He had been watching Penny as if he were trying to figure out how to do the same thing, and now he, too, began splashing with one front leg. The two of them were churning up enough water to wet everything within fifteen feet.

"Okay, who wants to *really* swim?" Leigh said. "Follow me—ponies last, please." She pressed Hot Shot forward to where the water began to get deeper. The others followed her out, until all at once the water was up to their waists and the horses' necks.

"Grab mane, and let the horses go where they want. Don't steer them unless you're getting too close to somebody," Leigh cautioned. "And this would not be a good time to fall off. Your horse might try to climb on top of you."

Megan had felt Pixie walking through the water. Then, suddenly, she felt her begin to swim. Megan grabbed mane and also hung on with her legs, since the water was lifting her off Pixie's back. She bent forward a little, trying to figure out how to stay with the unfamiliar motion.

"This is so cool!" she heard Max say.

The horses' "swimming" was really sort of like cantering in slow motion through the water. Once she got used to the motion, Megan began to enjoy it herself. She had never done anything like it. It was thrilling!

"Isn't this fun?" Chloe said.

"It's like flying," Megan replied.

The horses swam out a little way, then began turning back toward shore. In a few moments, Megan felt Pixie's feet find the bottom again as they "landed." Suddenly, she wasn't weightless anymore on Pixie's back, and she relaxed her hold on the mane.

"That was awesome!" Megan said.

"Let's do it again, Leigh, please?" Max said.

"Nope. It's tiring. Let them rest. And let's not push our luck, shall we? We're already two for five on the accidental dismounts. By the way, is anyone else planning to fall off today?" Leigh joked.

"Not me," Keith said.

"Me neither," Max added.

"I'm not planning on it," Chloe said. "But I'm not making any guarantees—"

Just as she finished speaking, Bo Peep decided to shake. She stuck her neck out and shook her whole body vigorously, just like a dog after a bath. Chloe slipped to one side, grabbed mane, pulled herself back up too hard, and fell off the other side, landing in the water just like Megan had.

"Make that three for five," Leigh said, rolling her eyes.

Everyone began to laugh again. Bo Peep snorted as if she were also amused. Chloe was laughing so hard she could hardly breathe. When she finally caught her breath, she grabbed a handful of mane and, with a grunt and a big jump, heaved herself up on Bo Peep's round back. But she hadn't counted on it being slippery. Before she could catch herself or get a leg over the pony, she slipped and fell head-first off the other side. She quickly stood up and wiped the water from her face.

If the first fall had been funny, the second one sent everyone into hysterics. Chloe had tears in her eyes, but she wasn't hurt. The tears were from laughing so hard. She went around to the pony's left side and tried again to get on. This time, she was weak and gasping from laughing so much, so it took four tries before she managed to haul herself up on Bo Peep's back. She finally dragged her right leg over and sat up slowly.

Leigh was shaking her head in disbelief. "I really thought I had seen all the ways a person could fall off a horse—but between Amanda, Megan, and Chloe, I've seen more entertaining and original ways to part company with a horse than I ever imagined!" She turned Hot Shot toward the shore and walked out of the water. "Come on, you four. It's about time to head back. Let's start getting your boots on."

By the time they had all put their socks and boots and helmets and chaps back on, the breeze had nearly dried the horses. They mounted up and headed back toward the gate. Megan's shirt was still damp, but it felt cool and pleasant.

The horses seemed relaxed from the swim, too. Pixie, who was usually a little "up," was walking along with her head low and her ears at half mast. Megan was enjoying being able to walk on a loose rein. Usually, she had to keep the reins gathered up, since Pixie could be a little spooky.

Penny and Popsicle were side by side, as usual. Keith looked over at Max and said, "Did you notice that all the people who fell off today were girls?"

"Hey, that's true," Max said. "I guess guys are just naturally better riders, right, Keith?" He put out a hand for Keith to high-five.

"Right," Keith said, reaching out to slap Max's hand. At that moment, Penny's saddle slid off to the side, and Keith landed on the ground with a thump, right on a big, prickly thistle.

"Ow!"

Megan and Chloe howled with laughter. "Oh, yeah, right," Megan said. "Guys are definitely much better riders than girls—if they can remember to get the cinch tight enough!"

Leigh turned around to see what had happened. Keith was sitting on a thistle. Penny stood beside him waiting patiently, her saddle hanging upside-down under her belly. *Here we go again*, her expression seemed to say.

"Another one bites the dust," Leigh sighed. "Keith,

how many times have you been told to check Penny's cinch again before you ride off?"

"About as many times as the saddle's slipped with me, I guess." Keith grinned. "Ouch!" He stood up, wincing, and began pulling stickers out of the seat of his pants.

Even Max had to laugh. "It looks like I'm the only one left. I wonder when I'm going to fall off."

"How about if you don't?" Leigh suggested.

"I'm not planning to," Max said, "but I guess you just never know."

Leigh dismounted and went to help Keith fix Penny's saddle. After he was on, she tightened the cinch again for him. "There," she said. "That ought to hold the saddle on. Think you can stay on top for a while?"

"Yes. Thanks, Leigh."

"Okay, let's get going. We'll have to hurry a little to get back in time."

They trotted on, heading back in the direction of the barn. As they came up over a hill, they spotted Jake down below. He was walking along with a bucket in one hand. Every so often, he would shake it, rattling the oats in the bottom.

"Hey, Jake!" Keith yelled. He waved enthusiastically.

Jake waved back and then headed up the hill toward them. "Y'all haven't seen that rogue of a horse, have you?" he yelled when he was close enough to be heard.

"You mean Prince Charming?" Keith shouted back. "Nope. We were just over by the lake, and we didn't see him anywhere."

When Jake reached the group, Megan could see he looked sweaty and annoyed. He set the bucket down and grumbled, "I almost had my hand on that dad-gum critter three times, and three times he turned and ran away from me before I could get him. I'm tempted to just leave him out here with all his tack on." Jake lifted his Braves baseball cap and wiped his face with his shirttail.

"If we see him, we'll try to get him to follow us back," Leigh said. "We've got to go on, or we'll be late. These guys are trying to make me the first trainer at Thistle Ridge ever to have a whole class fall off."

"Well, y'all be careful," Jake said. "I'm going to have one more try at catching that horse of the Sloanes, and if he runs away again, old Gerald Sloane'll just have to come out here and catch him himself." He put his cap back on, picked up the bucket of feed, and started down the hill.

"Chloe, can you imagine Mr. Sloane with his cigar and his suit and briefcase running after Prince Charming?" Megan said.

Chloe giggled. "Can you imagine how grouchy he'd be?"

" 'Amandasue, you make that horse of yours come here rat now!' " Megan lowered her voice and imitated Mr. Sloane's gravelly Southern drawl.

"What's that?" Chloe interrupted her.

Megan looked in the direction Chloe was looking. She saw a flash of white and heard a faint whinny. "It's Prince Charming!"

"Where?" Leigh asked.

"There." Megan pointed. "See him? He just went behind that big clump of brush."

Sure enough, in a moment, Prince Charming came out from behind the bushes. He was trotting with his tail held high and his nose up in the air, swinging his head from side to side as if he were looking for something. The reins dangled from the sides of the bit, the broken one short, the other dragging the ground. He whinnied again. Pixie answered him, but the wind was blowing in the wrong direction, so he didn't hear or smell the other horses. Prince trotted on across the ridge a hundred yards from them and headed down the other side.

"Think we should go after him?" Megan said.

Leigh sighed. She looked at her watch. "I guess we should. Jake was headed in the wrong direction. He'll never find him. All right. We're going to make one try to catch him, and if he runs away, we're going back without him. Come on."

They picked up a trot and headed out after Amanda's wayward horse. As soon as they came down the hill, Leigh let them canter a little so they'd catch up with him faster. At the top of the next hill, they spotted Prince's white hindquarters for a moment before he disappeared into the woods. They were much closer to him.

In the woods they had to slow down. Fortunately, the ground was still wet under the trees from the big storm the day before, so it was easy to follow Prince's footprints. In another moment, they came out of the trees and into a clearing.

"That's strange," Leigh said. She pulled up and waited for the others to reach her. "I never knew this was here."

Before them was an old barn. The gray oak of its wooden sides twisted weirdly, as if a giant hand from above had mashed it and turned it at the same time. There was something ominous about its gaping windows and doors and its sagging roof. It was overgrown on two sides by thick, broadleafed kudzu vines and honeysuckle. Megan could smell the dank, green kudzu mixed with the sweet honeysuckle. It looked darker inside the barn than it should have, considering the bright July sun was beating down on the rusty tin roof. The endless buzz of cicadas in the grass rose around them, grew louder, and then faded again. For some reason Megan shivered suddenly, in spite of the heat.

"Wow," Max said softly. "This place is creepy."

"You're not kidding," Megan said. "It looks haunted."

"I never even knew it was here," Keith said. "I wonder if Jake knows."

"Did anybody see where Prince Charming went?" Leigh asked.

Nobody was sure. The kids wanted to go inside the old barn, but Leigh decided they should head back. Glancing at her watch. She said, "Come on, kids. We really can't stay here right now. Besides, the barn looks dangerous. It looks like it might fall down any minute. I'm surprised it didn't blow over in that storm we had yesterday."

Reluctantly, they turned and followed Leigh. Just before they entered the woods, Megan pulled Pixie to a halt and looked back over her shoulder. She could see the old, wide barn door hanging off its hinges, and nothing but blackness beyond it.

Pixie began to shift her weight uneasily from foot to foot. Megan thought she was fretting that the other horses had left her behind, but her ears were pointed forward, toward the old barn. What was wrong with Pixie? Megan wondered. The pony seemed restless, even anxious.

Suddenly, Megan saw something move in the shadows behind the door, a flash of white against the dark inside. The sight of it sent a chill down her spine. She was sure it was a ghost!

5

MEGAN COULD HARDLY BELIEVE WHAT SHE'D JUST SEEN. She turned Pixie and headed back through the trees as fast as she could. Branches slapped against Megan's face as she urged Pixie on, but Megan barely noticed. She only knew she had to get away from the ghost. In her panicked state, she wasn't sure what direction she was headed in, but then she came around a turn in the path and was relieved to see Bo Peep's round rear trotting along up ahead.

"Chloe! Wait for me," Megan called, her heart pounding in her chest.

Chloe looked over her shoulder and saw Megan's frightened face. "What's the matter? You look like you just saw a ghost," she said, slowing Bo Peep so that Megan could catch up with her.

"I think maybe I did," Megan said breathlessly.

Then she told Chloe about the white figure she had seen flash by the barn door. "It had two long legs, and I'm sure I saw a face with big, dark eyes looking at me. Chloe, I never would have believed it if I hadn't seen it myself."

"Do you really think it was a ghost?" Chloe sounded doubtful. "My dad says there's no such thing as ghosts."

"Do I sound like I'm making this up?" Megan said. "I know there's not *supposed* to be any such thing as ghosts, but then what was it I saw?"

"A shadow, maybe?" Chloe guessed.

"Whoever heard of a white shadow with legs and a face and eyes?"

"Maybe it was the kudzu, then," Chloe said. "You know how it can look like people or weird shapes when the wind blows it."

Megan shook her head. "No way. What I saw wasn't kudzu," she insisted. "And it wasn't any shadow, either."

The rest of the way back, Megan was silent. But she couldn't help thinking about the ghost. After everyone untacked the horses and brushed them, Leigh called them into the courtyard. Jake was cooking hot dogs and hamburgers on the grill for their lunch.

"Excellent!" Keith said.

"I'm starving!" Max said.

They had been late getting back, so most of the kids had finished eating already. Besides hot dogs and hamburgers, there was cole slaw, potato salad, and corn on the cob. The four piled food on paper plates and went to sit under the shade of the massive pin oak tree that grew in the courtyard.

A group of the older kids sat nearby. Megan recognized Keith's sister, Haley, who was fourteen. Haley's black hair was cut fashionably short, except for one long lock that was wrapped with stripes of brightly colored thread. She also had five tiny silver loop earrings in one ear and a small diamond in the other. Megan thought Haley was really pretty. She watched Haley talking with the four other older kids, three girls she didn't know and a boy named Tyler Lamar, who kept a horse at Thistle Ridge.

Suddenly, Megan realized that Keith, Chloe, and Max were staring at her. "What?" she said.

"Megan, you're not even eating your lunch," Chloe said. "And Max just asked you a question. He said your name three times."

"Sorry," Megan said. She picked up her hot dog, which was now cold, and took a bite.

"We were talking about that old barn we saw in the back pasture. We think it would be fun to go over there and check it out. There might be all sorts of cool things in there—old tools and things," Keith said.

"I, um, I don't think I really want to go back there," Megan said. "Like Leigh said, it's probably not safe. I could fall down any second."

"Since when do you worry about safety, Miss Jump Without Supervision?" Max demanded. "That old barn has probably been there for a hundred years. It's not going to fall down all of a sudden."

"What barn?" It was Tyler Lamar, who had been sitting nearest them.

"There's this old barn on one of the hills over in the back pasture," Keith told him. "We came across it this morning when we were on our trail ride. I never saw it before."

"Oh, that old place. We've seen it plenty of times, right, Haley?" He winked at her.

"Sure," Haley said. "But I'd stay away from there if I were you," she added. "Everyone knows it's haunted."

"Haunted?" Megan gulped. She and Chloe exchanged looks.

"Haunted," Tyler agreed.

"It's haunted by the ghost of a girl who was killed in a fire," Haley explained in a hushed tone. "And she had this horse that she loved. She used to ride up the ridge every evening. People say she still goes back to the old barn where she used to spend so much time with her horse."

"How was she killed?" Chloe asked.

"Her parents went out to a party," Haley continued. "They left her all alone, except for the servants. When they came home, the house was on fire. No one could get in to rescue her. She didn't wake up until it was too late."

"How old was she?" Megan asked.

"How old are you?" Haley said.

"Eleven."

"That's what I thought," Haley said dramatically. "She was *exactly* your age."

"My age?" Megan whispered.

"Yes," Haley said. "And she was an only child. She used to ride out on her horse every evening, all alone, looking for someone to be friends with, until the night she was killed in the fire."

"No way," Keith said.

"Way," Haley said. "We've seen her, haven't we, Tyler?"

"Yeah," he said seriously. "I never would have believed it if I hadn't seen it myself. That poor girl in her long, white nightgown, looking for her horse—"

"—moaning and crying," Haley added.

"Cut it out, Haley," Keith said. "Nobody believes that stuff. You're just making it up to scare us."

Megan's eyes were wide. She was looking at Chloe. "Chloe, do you think . . . ?"

"It might have been," Chloe said somberly.

"It must have been," Megan said.

"Tell them," Chloe said.

Megan gulped. "Keith, she's not making it up. I saw it. I *saw* the ghost of the girl!"

"What did she look like?" Tyler asked.

"I saw her just as we were all leaving the barn," Megan recalled. "Everyone else was ahead of me, and I stopped to take one more look at the place. That's when I saw the ghost, inside the barn door. It was all in white, just like the girl in the nightgown. It was the scariest thing! It was her, I know it was!"

"Did she see you?" Haley wanted to know.

"I don't know. She could have—she was looking right in my direction. I could see her eyes. Why?" Megan asked, full of dread.

"Because if she saw you, she might come looking for you," Haley said ominously.

"Yeah, I'd be sure to sleep with your lights on, if I were you," Tyler said. He stood up. "I'm getting some more chocolate chip cookies. Anybody else want some?"

"Yeah, bring me one," Haley said.

"Me, too," Keith and Max said together.

Tyler went off in the direction of the picnic table, where all the food was. Megan tried another bite of hot dog, but it was hard to swallow. She couldn't stop thinking about the story of the girl who had been killed in the fire.

"Haley?" Megan said softly, hoping the others wouldn't hear.

"Yeah?"

"You don't really think the ghost would come looking for me, do you?"

"Oh, come on, Megan," Max scoffed. "You know there's no such thing as ghosts. Quit being such a baby."

"I'm not a baby, *little* brother," Megan retorted. "I know what I saw. How else can you explain it?"

"I'm sure you saw something. But whatever it

was, it wasn't a ghost," Max scoffed. "It was probably just the sunlight playing tricks on your eyes."

"There's one way to find out," Chloe said. "We go back up to the barn and take a look. Whatever Megan saw should still be there. And if we can't find anything that could explain it, then maybe we have to believe her."

"Chloe's right," Keith said. "We ought to at least check it out."

"Megan?" Max said. "What do you say?"

They were all looking at her. Megan twisted her paper napkin and looked away, toward the woods. The last thing she wanted to do was go back to the old barn. She was sure she had seen the ghost girl Haley and Tyler had described. But if she didn't go, no one would believe her story, and she'd look like a chicken. And anyway, maybe they'd be right—maybe they'd find some logical explanation for what she had seen. At least she wouldn't be alone. Whatever happened, it would happen to all of them.

"I guess I'll go," Megan said.

"Good. When?" Keith said.

"We can't go 'til later," Max reminded them. "We have arts and crafts after lunch, and then we're supposed to have a jump lesson."

"So we'll go after the jump lesson," Keith said. "There will still be enough daylight then."

"I sure hope so," Megan muttered.

"You guys don't know what you're talking about," Haley said. "You're going to get the pants scared off you." She lowered her voice to make the words seem

54

serious. "Tyler and I have been to that barn. And we've seen the ghost, too. Luckily, she didn't see us, and we were able to escape. But the next people to see her might not be so lucky. They just . . . might . . ."

"DIE!" a voice shrieked, and at the same instant, Megan felt something grab her shoulders. She screamed before she could stop herself.

Haley and the older girls were rolling on the ground laughing. Keith and Max were howling. It was Tyler who had snuck up behind Megan, yelled, and grabbed her shoulders. With a smirk, Tyler went over and sat by Haley. He had obviously enjoyed scaring the daylights out of Megan.

"Tyler Lamar, that was mean," Chloe said indignantly. "You ought to be ashamed of yourself."

"Anyone who would believe such a lame story deserves to have the pee scared out of them," Tyler said, stuffing a cookie into his mouth.

"Oh, yeah? Well, it you're so brave, why don't you come with us?" Megan demanded. "We're going to the barn after camp. That way, we can find out just exactly what it was that I saw. And if we don't find anything, then I say you'll have to believe me."

"Sure thing, kid," Tyler said casually. "Haley and I'll come to the big, scary barn with you, won't we, Haley?"

"Sure," Haley said. "After all, you're going to need all the protection you can get. That ghost is going to be looking for you!" She and Tyler began laughing again.

"All right," Megan said. "Meet us at the pasture gate as soon as you get done with your last ride."

"See ya, wouldn't want to be ya," Tyler said. He and Haley got up and went inside.

"Do you think we ought to tell Jake we're going?" Megan said nervously.

"No, let's not tell him," Keith said. "He might not let us go. We'll check it out first and then ask him if he knows about the place."

"Did he ever catch Prince Charming? If he didn't, we ought to tell him where we saw him last," Chloe reminded them.

"I heard him say he would go out at feeding time and try again," Keith said. "I guess he figures Prince'll show up when he gets hungry."

"Let's take a bucket of feed and try to catch him ourselves," Megan said. "Then we can say we were out looking for him, if anyone questions us."

"Good idea, Meg," Max said.

They spent the next couple of hours making leather bracelets. They used leather engraving tools to print the names of their favorite horses on the bracelets. Then they got to paint the letters with a special leather dye. Megan already had a bracelet with "Pixie" engraved on the brass nameplate, so she decided to make one that said "Paddington," her favorite school horse at her old barn in Connecticut.

After arts and crafts, it was time to tack up the horses again for their lesson in the ring. Leigh made a "gymnastic" for them out of three small jumps in a row. She made them tie up their reins so the horses couldn't step in them, then they had to jump all the jumps with their eyes closed and their arms held out to the side.

Megan usually liked working on balance exercises, but this time she couldn't relax. She was nervous about returning to the old barn, and she couldn't stop thinking about the ghost. She wondered if they would see it again.

Finally, the lesson was over. As soon as they took care of the horses, the kids went down the hill to the pasture gate. Haley and Tyler were the last to arrive. When they got there, the sun was dropping toward one of the ridges beyond the pasture.

"Do you think we'll make it there and back before it gets dark?" Megan asked nervously.

"If we go now, we will," Tyler said. "Come on, you wimps. Let's go find your ghost."

6

THE SIX KIDS CLIMBED OVER THE FENCE AND HURRIED toward the woods, hoping they wouldn't be seen. As they passed the tree that had been struck by lightning, Megan saw that the bigger half of it was leaning to one side now, slowly uprooting itself. Once they were out of sight of the barn they could slow down. They stepped through the knee-high grass, talking and laughing. In the long shadows on the east side of the hill it was cool and pleasant after the heat of the day.

Megan trudged along, swinging the feed bucket. Occasionally, she lifted it up and gave it a shake, hoping the familiar rattle would attract Prince Charming. Max and Keith were in the lead. Suddenly, they both stopped and threw out their arms wide. Megan bumped right into Max and nearly fell down.

"Ouch! Max! What are you doing!"

"Sssh!" Max cautioned. He pointed toward the crest of the hill.

"It's Jake! Get down," Tyler hissed.

They all crouched low in the tall grass. Jake was walking toward the top of the ridge, carrying a feed bucket and a halter and lead line, looking for Prince Charming. In another minute, they would have run into him.

"This way," Tyler whispered, motioning for them to follow. They began to skirt the bottom of the hill, crouching low and running from one clump of brambles to the next, hoping Jake wouldn't see them.

At last, they made it around the base of the hill. Tyler stood up. Megan and the others did, too. Megan's back ached from crouching for so long, and her arm was tired from holding the feed bucket. She set it down and rubbed at the muscle.

"Jake was headed over that way," Tyler said. "If we keep to this side of the hill, we should be able to avoid running into him. It just means it'll take a little longer to get to the barn. It's in those woods up there, on top of that ridge. We'll have to go around to the backside of the hill and come at it from behind. Come on," he said.

"Anyone else feel like carrying the bucket for a while?" said Megan hopefully.

Max picked up the bucket and followed Tyler. It took them another fifteen minutes to get to the backside of the hill. The sun was sinking above the highest ridge in the next pasture. Soon it would be getting dark. Glad she wasn't alone, Megan followed the rest of the group into the deepening shadows of the woods.

The western slope of the ridge was much steeper than they had thought. In some places, they had to pull themselves up with vines and branches. Finally, the slope became more gradual. In another minute, they came out of the trees and into the clearing where the old barn stood.

The first time Megan had seen it was in broad daylight. Even then, it had looked forbidding. It was even more spooky in the fading evening light. Thick, green kudzu vines crept from the trees and covered two sides of the barn, as if trying to claim it as part of the woods. A bit of breeze touched the broad leaves, making them rustle a little, but they looked as if they might move on their own.

Beyond the sagging doors and windows of the barn, it was utterly black. Megan peered into the darkness, which seemed to be bottomless, and wondered if the ghost was hiding inside. Was it watching her right now?

The old barn had stood silent and untouched on this ridge for a hundred years. Megan had the feeling that it had been waiting all that time, for someone to come and hear its secrets. She couldn't help feeling it had something to say. She stared at it, half expecting it to speak.

Just then, a whippoorwill began its mournful, three-note trill. Lightning bugs began to blink in the shadows at the edge of the woods. Tyler spoke, startling them all. Max dropped the feed bucket and quickly bent to pick it up. Embarrassed, he shoved it at Megan. She took it absently from him, unable to stop staring at the barn.

"Well, come on, you wussies," Tyler said, walking toward the barn. "Let's go find your ghost."

He went about twenty feet before he turned around and saw that no one was following him. In fact, no one had budged an inch from where they stood. Tyler stopped and scowled at them, his hands on his hips. "Are y'all coming or not?"

The other kids all looked at each other, not wanting to admit they were scared to go into the barn, now that it was getting so dark. Even Haley hesitated. The sky had turned pale purple, with a few streaky red clouds reflecting the low sun. The inside of the barn was as dark as midnight. The endless chant of the cicadas rose and fell, rose and fell, in the softening light.

"I wish we had brought a flashlight," Chloe said.

"Maybe we should just come back when it's light again," Megan said nervously.

"We're not really going to find a ghost in there, guys. Get real! Now are you coming with me or not?" Tyler demanded.

Reluctantly, they followed him up to the barn door. One of the big double doors was closed. The other was halfway open. Tyler tried to pull it open more, but weeds had grown up around the bottom of it so that it wouldn't budge. He gave it a kick with the heel of his boot.

"Well, who's going in first?" Tyler said.

"You are," Megan said.

Tyler laughed. "All right. But you're coming with me."

Megan started to protest, but Tyler grabbed her by the wrist and pulled her toward the doorway. Just as he did, the cicadas stopped singing. The silence was eerie. A whippoorwill called again, from somewhere close by. Megan jumped.

"We're all coming with you, right, guys?" Max said.

"Right," Keith said.

Chloe nodded. "We're in this together."

"Absolutely," Haley added.

"Okay," Megan said. She took a deep breath. The old barn, or whatever was inside it, seemed to be waiting for them to enter. "Here we go," she said, and stepped into the gloom.

Tyler was still holding on to her wrist, but she was glad. She couldn't see anything at all. They all stood close together, just inside the door, waiting for their eyes to get used to the light. Megan smelled a peculiar, damp, earthy smell, which was vaguely familiar. And faintly, underneath it, the smell of horse. That was a good smell. She wondered how it could linger after so many years.

"See anything?" Haley asked.

"It's too dark," Tyler said.

Then Megan heard something—a scuffling sound

and a soft thump, as if a body had brushed up against a wall. She froze.

"Did you hear that?" Megan peered into the gloom, her eyes wide, trying to see what could have made the noise.

"What was it?" Chloe said in a loud whisper.

"Probably just a RAT!" Tyler said, trying to scare her.

"There can't be rats in here," Max said. "What would they eat?"

"Bodies," Tyler said.

"Cut it out, Tyler," Keith said.

"Are we just going to stand here in the doorway or what?" Haley said impatiently.

"I'm waiting for my eyes to adjust," Megan said.

"If they're not adjusted by now, you can pretty much close them," Max said. "It's not getting any lighter in here."

The only light at all came from two windows on one wall. Through them, the pale twilight seeped in, barely outlining the rough plank wall. The other windows had been boarded up or were covered with kudzu. Tyler started walking toward the opposite end of the barn. It was about fifty feet to the end, but they couldn't see even half that far. They took small, scuffling steps, with their arms outstretched, hoping they wouldn't bump into anything.

"We should have brought a flashlight," Tyler muttered.

"I don't think we're going to find anything," Megan said hopefully.

Just then, she heard a sound. She stopped in midstep. "What's that?" Megan whispered.

It was coming straight toward them, growing louder—step, step, step, step. Then they saw it. It appeared in the soft, blue light from one of the windows—a tall, white figure, with two dark eyes staring down at them. It made a low sound.

For one second Megan was absolutely paralyzed with fright. Then she screamed like she never had before.

"Ruuun!" Tyler yelled. They all bolted for the pale rectangle of light that was the open door.

The six of them all tripped over each other getting out, then nobody seemed to know which way to run. "That way!" Tyler yelled, pointing toward the woods in the direction of the main barn.

Megan was still clutching the feed bucket. She was running as fast as she could. She was so frightened she didn't seem to be able to draw a breath. But at the same time, she was elated that they had all seen the ghost! Now they would have to believe her.

She glanced over her shoulder to see if the others were behind her. She didn't see anyone. Had she come the wrong way? Where did they all go? Would the ghost come after her, now that she was all alone? She ran harder. She could barely see the path. She came around a bend and ran right smack into something—something that grabbed her!

She screamed again, dropping the feed bucket. Whatever it was grasped her by the arms. She kicked wildly and tried to strike at it with her pinned arms. "MAAAX!" she screamed. "MAAAX, HEEELP!" Whatever held her now covered her mouth so she couldn't call out anymore.

"MEGAN!" said a familiar voice. "Stop that hollerin'!"

Then she realized who was holding her. She stopped kicking and felt the grip on her relax. "Jake?" she said.

"Yes, it's Jake, honey. What in the world are you doin' out here this late in the evenin'? What's got you so scared?"

"Oh, Jake! I've never been so glad to see anyone in my life!" Now that the worst of the scare was over, she started to cry. Jake put an arm around her shoulders and patted her awkwardly.

"Honey, what's the matter? Try and tell me what happened." Megan couldn't see his face anymore, but his voice was full of concern.

"We were at the old barn. And we saw—we saw—"

"Saw what?"

"Jake, it was a ghost! The ghost of the little girl who died in the fire! She was dressed in white, just like in the story! We saw her, really and truly!"

Jake listened as Megan told how she'd seen the ghost first and no one had believed her. Then she told him how they'd all come back to try and find out what was really in the old barn. "And this time we all saw it! They'll have to believe me now, won't they?" she finished.

"Where are the others?" Jake asked.

"I don't know. When the ghost came toward us, we all just ran away as fast as we could."

"Well, I reckon they can make it back all right. They shouldn't have left you, though. You say Tyler was with you? Where is he?"

Megan had to think for a moment. Then she told Jake she remembered seeing him start into the woods ahead of the rest of them, with Haley. "He must be back at the stables by now. He was running really fast."

"Meg?" a voice called from several yards away.

Megan recognized her brother's voice. "Max! I'm over here!" she shouted in great relief.

In a moment, Max came out of the trees. Chloe and Keith were with him. "Meg! Are you okay? All of a sudden you weren't with us, then Chloe heard you scream. We've been looking for you."

"I'm glad you're all right," Chloe said. "We were worried about you, after we saw the—" She broke off. "Did you tell Jake?"

"About the ghost?" Jake said. "Yeah, she told me. I want y'all to come with me. And stay together," he warned them. They followed him through the trees. By now, it was so dark in the woods they couldn't see the path under their feet, but Jake seemed to know the way instinctively. They were soon back in the clearing where the old barn stood.

"What'd you bring us back here for, Jake?" Keith

wanted to know. "I never ran away from anything so fast in my life, and I'm sure not in any hurry to meet that thing again, whatever it was."

"Yeah, Jake, can't we go? I'm really scared," Megan said.

"I want y'all to wait right here for just a minute," Jake said. "I'll be right back."

"Where are you going?"

"Into the barn."

"No way, man! Jake, don't do it!" Keith warned him. "I'm telling you, there's really a ghost in there."

"Stay here," Jake said, starting for the barn.

Speechless, they stood at the edge of the clearing and watched him disappear into the darkness inside the old barn. For several endless seconds, there was not a sound. Megan found Max's hand and held it very tightly. Her heart was pounding so loud she was sure everyone could hear it. Then there was a scuffling noise from inside the barn, and the sound of Jake's voice, but it was too muffled for them to make out what he was saying.

"Do you think he's okay?" Keith's voice was anxious.

"I don't know," Max said.

"I sure hope so," Chloe said.

"Do you think we should go in after him?" Keith asked.

No one said anything. No sound came from inside the barn.

"I can't stand this," Keith said. "I'm going in after him."

"He told us to wait here," Chloe reminded him.

"I don't care! He must be in trouble," Keith insisted. "The ghost must've done something to him. I gotta help him!"

"I'll come with you," Max said.

"Max, no!" Megan held on to his hand. "We should go for help! Don't go in there."

Just then, a figure emerged from the dark barn doorway. It was Jake.

"Jake!" Keith said, relieved.

A tall white figure with two big eyes moved right beside him. Megan gasped.

"Here's your ghost, kids," Jake said.

Megan's mouth dropped open as she stared in amazement. Max began to laugh. The "ghost" was Prince Charming!

7

"I CAN'T BELIEVE I SPENT THE WHOLE DAY TRAIPSIN' ALL over this farm looking for this dad-gum horse that hasn't got sense enough to come home for his supper, and all the time he was right here in this ol' barn!" Jake shook his head. Then he grinned at them. "He sure gave y'all a scare, though, didn't he?"

"Boy, am I glad it was Prince Charming all the time," Megan said, patting the big horse's neck. "Even if he did scare us half to death, at least he wasn't a real ghost." She shuddered, remembering how frightened she'd been.

"We ought to be heading back now," Jake said. "Did any of you tell anybody you were coming out here? Does Sharon or Leigh know?"

"No," Max admitted. "We were afraid they wouldn't let us come, and we wanted to look for the ghost, or whatever Megan thought was the ghost."

"Well, they'll be good and worried about you by now, then," Jake said. "I imagine you'll have some explaining to do when we get back."

The moon had risen, bright and nearly full, so it was easy to see their way back to the stables. For a while, nobody spoke. Megan tramped through the grass, listening to the nighttime sounds of the farm. Lightning bugs blinked green all around them. Keith and Max were catching them and squashing them, then decorating themselves with the glowing green tails.

"Max, check it out." Keith had made a glowing bracelet across the top of his wrist from the squashed tails.

"Cool," Max said.

"That's terrible," Chloe scolded them. "Lightning bugs are living creatures, too. You shouldn't just kill them like that."

"Yeah," Megan said. "How would you feel if someone squashed you and made a necklace out of your butt?"

There was a pause, then Max and Keith started to laugh. Then Megan started to giggle, too, but she was trying not to, so it came out as sort of a snort. Even Chloe had to laugh at that. Max and Keith did stop squishing lightning bugs, though.

When they got back to the barn, Sharon Wyndham was waiting for them. She always wore boots and breeches and kept her blond hair neatly pulled back in a ponytail. She stood in the aisle, her arms folded, and looked at the four children.

Megan couldn't seem to get her eyes above Sharon's perfectly fitted custom field boots. Sharon was one of the people Megan cared most about impressing. She couldn't figure out why she always seemed to mess up right when Sharon was around to see it!

"Well?" Sharon said. "What do you have to say for yourselves?"

Nobody spoke. "Your parents are waiting for you in the office," Sharon said. "They've been waiting for quite some time. They sent you to camp and trusted your care to me. How do you think it made me look when your parents came to pick you up and I couldn't tell them where any of you were?"

"We're sorry," Max said.

"We snuck away after camp to go to the old barn," Megan said. "You didn't have anything to do with it. We'll take all the blame."

"That's not the point," Sharon said. "The fact is, I am to blame. But from now on, when camp is going on, I expect you to be *where* you're supposed to be, *when* you're supposed to be there. And when camp hours are over, there'll be no going anyplace without checking in with an adult first. Understood?"

"Yes," Megan said.

"We won't do it again," Max added.

"You'd better not. If it happens again, you won't be allowed to attend camp, and I'll have to restrict your barn time," Sharon warned. "Okay. Go on into the office. I'm done lecturing you; now your parents get to have a turn!" Her tone had become just as friendly as it had been serious a minute ago. That was one of the best things about Sharon, Megan thought. When she was disappointed in you, you knew it right away, but as soon as you worked it out, she always forgave you and things got right back to normal.

At lunch the next day, Max, Megan, Keith, and Chloe were sitting under the big tree in the courtyard talking about the ghost that had turned out to be Prince Charming.

"I'm sure glad it wasn't a real ghost after all," Megan said, biting into a piece of fruit.

"Oh, yeah, we heard you finally figured out who your ghost was. I bet you felt dumb."

Megan turned to see that it was Tyler talking. He sat nearby on the grass, along with Haley and a couple of the bigger kids.

"You ran away faster than anybody, Tyler, remember?" Max said.

"I was just trying to scare you," Tyler said. "I knew it was the horse all the time."

"Oh, yeah, right," Keith said. "That's why you screamed the loudest and beat us all back to the barn."

"That's right." Tyler stomped on his empty soda can and kicked it at Keith. "Sure scared you, didn't I?" The big kids went off together, laughing and talking.

"It was sort of fun, wasn't it?" Megan said.

They all agreed that even when they had been scared, the whole thing had been a great adventure. And for some reason, Megan still felt curious about the old barn.

"Wouldn't it be fun to go on a trail ride at night?" Megan said.

"Yeah!" Max said.

"That would be so cool!" Keith agreed.

"Do you think they'd let us?" Chloe asked, sitting up.

"Maybe we could go on a trail ride and camp out overnight somewhere," Keith suggested.

"At the old barn!" Max said.

"Won't that be kind of scary?" Chloe said, hugging her knees.

"Now that we know there's not really a ghost, it won't be," Max said.

"How do we know for sure there's not really a ghost?" Megan asked.

"We don't, I guess," Max admitted with a shrug.

"Then it'll be just scary enough," Keith said excitedly.

"Now we just have to convince someone to take us," Max reminded them.

"Who do you think would do it?" Megan asked.

The four of them all thought for a minute, and they all came up with the same answer at once. "JAKE!" they shouted together. Then they jumped up and went to look for him.

Jake listened silently to their idea about taking a moonlight trail ride and camping out at the old barn. "Well," he said finally. "I can't see any harm in it. I don't mind taking y'all, if you can get Leigh to come, too."

Leigh agreed to come along on the trail ride with them. Then they had to convince Sharon. They thought she might say no, after their escapade in the pasture the night before, but, to their surprise, she readily agreed. "It sounds like fun to me," Sharon said. "But just remember—this is still part of the summer camp program, so all the campers in your group must be included. Do you know what I'm talking about?"

"Amanda," Chloe and Megan said at the same time.

"Yes. Now, I know she's sometimes not as easy to get along with as you'd like, but I want you all to make more of an effort to include her. Mrs. Sloane spoke to me about what happened on the trail ride yesterday. She told me that Bo Peep kicked Amanda's horse." She frowned at Chloe. "I want you all to be more responsible."

"But, Sharon, that's not what happened at all," Megan protested. "Amanda let Prince Charming run right into her!"

"I'm not interested in who's to blame. I don't want anybody else getting kicked. And I want you to try and find ways to be friendly to Amanda. All right?"

Reluctantly, they all promised to try and be nice to Amanda. The trail-ride campout was set for that Friday night. All week, they talked excitedly about it. They planned to build a campfire and roast hot dogs and marshmallows. Then they were going to tell ghost stories!

On Friday afternoon, they loaded up their stuff in Jake's old blue pickup, and he drove it out to the campsite. Earlier that day, he'd taken the tractor out with the big mower attachment and cut the grass short on the hilltop. At last, it was time to go on the trail ride!

The horses seemed puzzled to find themselves going out after their dinner. *Where are you taking me?* Pixie's expression said when Megan began putting on the saddle.

Jake came through the barn leading Buster, his big sorrel quarter horse. He was a handsome, dark, honey-brown color with a wavy, flaxen mane and tail and a little white star between his eyes. Buster was a cutting horse. Jake sometimes showed him in local shows, where Buster would set on a cow and cut her out of a herd. When Jake showed Buster, they almost always came away with a first-place trophy.

When they all were gathered outside the barn, Allie came by to do a safety check on their tack and to see them off. She took an extra minute to tighten Penny's cinch for Keith, shaking her head when she saw how loose it was. "I declare, Keith, it's a wonder you ever stay on this mare for more'n a minute."

"I just stay in the middle, Allie," Keith said. "Most

of the time," he added, remembering his most recent tumble.

"Well, y'all have fun. And let me know if you run across any more ghosts!"

Soon they were walking through the moonlit pastures of Thistle Ridge Farm. The breeze that blew across the ridge all day had died down, leaving the humid air still. Frogs and crickets chirped all around them, replacing the daytime song of the cicadas. Megan was thinking how odd it was that a place that was so familiar in the daylight could seem so different at night.

None of the kids had ever gone riding at night. Megan was thinking that anything that was fun to do in the daytime was always even more exciting at night. The horses seemed to enjoy it, too. Pixie was calmly walking along with her ears forward and her nose down. Even Prince Charming was minding his manners for a change. He ambled along behind Popsicle without bothering anyone or stopping to graze.

"The moon's so bright you could read by it," Max said.

"This is even better than swimming the horses in the lake," Megan said.

"Let's go see the lake," Keith said. "Can we, Jake?"

"Fine with me," Jake said.

The lake was still, except for an occasional ripple as a fish broke the surface looking for food. They let the horses drink, then rode around the shore. In the middle of the lake was a wavy image of the moon, which seemed to follow them as they made their way around the edge.

They trotted away from the lake, then cantered up a gently sloping hillside. At the top of the hill, they stopped to look at the beautiful view of the moonlit farm spreading around them on all sides. Then they began walking in the direction of the old barn, where they were going to spend the night.

Megan found herself near Amanda. "How are your scratches, Amanda?" she asked, trying to be friendly.

"Oh, they were terrible, just awful," Amanda replied. "I could hardly sleep, they stung so much."

"I bet that hurt," Megan said.

"Oh, it was dreadful. My mother says she hopes they don't leave permanent scars. She took me to a plastic surgeon already, just in case." Amanda sounded pleased.

"Well, you can hardly see that one on your face anymore," Megan said. "I never heard of anyone needing plastic surgery from getting scratched by briars."

"You might look good with a scar or two, Amanda," Keith said helpfully.

"Really? What do you think, Max?" Amanda asked eagerly.

"About what?"

"How do you think I look?"

"Huh? What do you mean? You look like a girl," Max stammered.

"Why, thank you, Max," Amanda gushed, as if

he'd just paid her a big compliment. "You are such a gentleman. You really must come over for dinner one night."

"Jake, can we canter again?" Max said quickly.

"No need to," Jake replied. "We're here."

They came to the top of a hill and saw the old barn standing in the clearing at the edge of the woods. Megan felt a little thrill go through her body, remembering the scary adventure they'd had when they'd thought Prince Charming was the ghost. She still felt mysteriously drawn to the old barn. "What's going to happen next?" she wondered as they rode up to the campsite.

8

BEHIND THE BARN WAS AN OLD PADDOCK, WHERE THEY turned out the horses for the night. Megan, Max, and their friends broke bales of hay into sections and threw them into the paddock, making a few separate piles so the horses wouldn't fight with each other.

When the horses had been taken care of, Jake lit the pile of brush and wood he'd gathered that afternoon. Soon the campfire was crackling busily, sending orange sparks up into the hazy blue of the nighttime sky. The campers sat around, eating the hot dogs they'd roasted on unbent coat hangers. Megan pulled her boots off and sat happily chugging a root beer and munching on a hot dog with lots of mustard. "This is my favorite meal," she announced, wiggling her toes with pleasure.

"Wait'll you have dessert," Chloe said.

"What's for dessert?"

"S'mores!" Chloe sang out.

"Yum!" Megan said, finishing the rest of her hot dog. "What are we waiting for? Let's have them now!"

They toasted marshmallows over the campfire and then made gooey sandwiches with the graham crackers and chocolate bars they'd brought. When they'd all eaten as much as they could hold, they began telling ghost stories.

Megan had suggested that they each come prepared to tell a story, so they took turns telling the scariest stories they knew. Keith told a Native American story about a boy who fought a spirit that was making his tribe suffer. Max told a story his grandmother had told him, about the ghost of a black pony that carried away some children. Megan also told one of her grandmother's tales. Max and Megan's grandmother had grown up in Ireland, right in the middle of horse country, and knew all sorts of wonderful and spooky tales. When it was Chloe's turn, she came up with a story about an animal ghost who saved the lives of the family who owned him. Everybody thought her story was the best. Then it was Amanda's turn, but she said she didn't know any ghost stories.

"Jake, you tell one," Keith said.

"Yeah! You tell us a ghost story," Megan said.

"Come on, Jake, let's hear it," Keith said.

"Okay. I've got one for you. But you have to get

yourselves all ready to go to sleep before I tell it," Jake said.

They all unrolled their sleeping bags and laid them out around the campfire, which had burned down to a glowing mound of sticks. They were all sleeping in their clothes, except Amanda, who had changed into a long nightgown. Over her nightgown, she was wearing a robe with little pink flowers all over it. On her feet were furry slippers that matched the pink in the robe. Megan stared at her in amazement when she came out of the cab of Jake's truck, where she had gone to change.

"Amanda, what on earth are you wearing?" Megan asked.

"Why, my night clothes, of course. Why?" Amanda replied airily.

"This is a *campout*. You're not supposed to wear a *nightgown* on a *campout*."

"Why not?"

"Well . . . because . . . it just doesn't seem right," Megan said lamely. "Haven't you ever been camping before?"

"Well, of course I have. My parents took me camping at the Grand Canyon last summer. We stayed in a lovely hotel with the best view of the canyon."

"Amanda, if you stayed in a fancy hotel, that wasn't camping," Keith pointed out.

"My daddy said we were camping in style," Amanda said with a shrug.

Jake laughed. "That sounds just like your daddy, Amanda. Are y'all about ready to settle down now?"

"Yes," Amanda said, plopping down on her sleeping bag.

"We're ready to hear your ghost story, Jake," Keith said.

"Yeah, let's hear it," Leigh said.

"It's not too scary is it?" Megan asked.

"Megan!" Max said. "A ghost story is *supposed* to be scary! If you don't want to listen, then cover your ears."

"I know, I know," Megan said. "It's just . . . we're so close to the barn. The door's open, and it's right behind me. Wait a minute." She got up, took her sleeping bag, and moved over to the opposite side of the campfire, next to Leigh. She spread out her sleeping bag again, and lay down. "There. That's better. Okay, go ahead, Jake."

"All right. Are y'all ready to listen?" Jake said.

"Wait," Chloe said. She had been on the other side of the fire, next to Megan. She picked up her stuff and moved it over, squeezing in between Megan and Leigh. "Okay, sorry, Jake. Go ahead."

"Now, before I start, is anyone else going to move their sleeping bags?" he asked.

Nobody said anything. Max and Keith were also near the barn. They looked through the half-open door at the pitch-black inside of the barn. Then they looked at each other in the dim orange glow from the fire. Without a word, they picked up their sleeping bags and went around to the other side of the fire, dumping their stuff on either side of Jake. He waited for them to get settled, then he began.

"Over a hundred years ago, these hills looked pretty much the same as they do now. My family has worked this land for three generations, and it was farmland for years before that. Now, back in those days, more than a hundred fifty years ago, there was a family who owned this land and much of the neighboring land for miles around. Dellbrook, their name was. They lived in a big white plantation house on top of one of these hills. They were wealthy and had slaves to help raise their cattle and crops.

"Mr. Dellbrook was a good businessman and soon made more money than he could spend in those days. He married a Quaker woman he met on business in Pennsylvania and brought her down to live on the plantation. After a while, they had a daughter.

"Old Dellbrook was good to his wife and child. He bought his daughter a fancy pony and taught her to ride. They used to ride up and down the ridges in the evening when his business was finished. The girl loved her pony and used to go down to the pasture every night to see him before she went to bed.

"But as good as Old Dellbrook was to his family, he was a terrible slave owner. He was away on business often and had hired a mean old overseer who beat the slaves to make them work harder. The slaves all hated the overseer. Once they made a plan to kill him, but Dellbrook found out about it. He rounded up the slaves who were involved in the plot and sent them south on the chain gang, where they'd never see their families again. Then the rest of the slaves were too afraid to do anything. They just worked and suffered under the mean overseer's whip.

"One night, there was a terrible storm. The Dellbrooks had gone out to a party and left their daughter at home with the servants. Lightning struck the house, and it caught on fire. The girl was trapped in the house."

Just then, a loud pop from the campfire sent out sparks, and Megan jumped. She looked up to see countless orange sparkles flying up toward the black sky. Her heart raced as she looked over at Chloe, whose green eyes had grown big and round.

"A slave saw the fire and went to try to rescue the girl," Jake continued. "She was beating on the windows, trying to get someone to come and save her. The slave couldn't get to her from inside the house, because the staircase was already on fire, so he climbed up the outside of the house toward the girl's window.

"About that time, the overseer heard the commotion of the servants who'd escaped the burning house. He saw the fire and thought that the slaves were having a rebellion. So he grabbed his gun and went after the slave climbing up the side of the house, not realizing that the slave was only trying to save the girl. The two men reached a narrow ledge outside the girl's window. Everyone watched as they struggled, both trying to get the gun. Suddenly, a shot rang out, and both men disappeared. To this day, no one knows if they were killed or if one or both of them climbed down somehow and escaped. The house burned to the ground. The girl was never rescued; she died in the fire.

"Now, they say that on many evenings, you can see the ghost of the girl walk out to the fence where she used to stand and pat her horse. And on stormy nights, the ghost of the slave comes back and stalks the grounds of the old house, trying to rescue the trapped girl."

There was silence. Heat lightning flashed in the eastern sky. The campfire was just a pile of glowing ashes.

"That was a great story, Jake," Keith said.

"Is that really true?" Megan wanted to know.

"Well, it surely is true that there were plantations with slaves around here," Jake explained. "And it's also true that some people, especially the Quakers, risked their own lives to help the slaves to escape. You know about the Underground Railroad, right? My daddy told that story to me when I was about your age," Jake went on. "He always swore it was true. I don't know if it was true or not, but I know there was once a house up on the ridge next to this one. I've found pieces of broken china and old bottles and things there."

"Maybe that's where the locket I found came from!" Megan said excitedly. "I'll bet it belonged to someone who lived in that house."

"Now, that may be so, Megan," Jake said.

"So far, no one's claimed it. I hope I get to keep it," Megan said.

"Jake, did you ever see the ghosts of the girl and the slave?" Keith asked.

"No, I can't say I have," Jake replied.

"Do you think there're really such things as ghosts?" Megan asked.

"Do you?" Jake said.

"Well . . . I sure thought I was seeing a ghost in the old barn. Then it turned out to be Prince Charming. I guess there's probably a logical explanation for it whenever people think they see a ghost."

"People sometimes believe what they want to," Leigh said.

"Do you want to believe that there are ghosts?" Jake asked.

Megan thought for a minute. Then she looked at the big, silent old barn standing in the moonlight. "Not tonight!" she said.

Everyone laughed at that. They stayed awake awhile longer, talking and telling more stories. Then, pretty soon, they began dropping off to sleep. Megan made herself one more s'more. When she had finished the last gooey bite, she licked the chocolate from her fingers and lay down. "Chloe," she whispered.

"Hmm," Chloe said sleepily.

"Are you asleep?"

"Yes," Chloe said. "Why?"

"I was just thinking," Megan said. "What if it really was the ghost of the girl I saw in the barn the other day?"

"Megan, we all saw it, remember? It turned out to be Prince Charming."

Megan propped herself up on one elbow. "I know that *night* it was Prince Charming. But how do we know it was Prince that I saw in the barn earlier that day? How do we know it wasn't the ghost?"

"Didn't it look the same?"

"Well, sort of, but I only got a glimpse of it during the day. I couldn't be sure."

"Well, I guess there's really no way to know for sure." Chloe yawned. "Just try not to think about it."

"Try not to think about ghosts when I'm out in the middle of nowhere right next to an old barn that I already think I saw a ghost in?" Megan muttered, lying down again. "Okay. No problem. I'll just think about slaves getting murdered. Or people being killed when lightning strikes their house and it burns down. Nice, cheerful thoughts like that."

She stared at the full, round moon overhead. A smoky finger of cloud poked its way across the moon, cutting it into silvery halves. As she watched, the finger widened until it covered the moon completely. Megan closed her eyes so she couldn't see how dark it had become. Somewhere in the distance, she heard the soft grumble of thunder. "Oh, great," she said to herself. "I sure hope we don't get caught out here in a storm like the one the other day." Then she began to drift off.

She woke up suddenly and swiped at her face in alarm. Something had been touching her. She could hardly see anything, and for several seconds she couldn't think where she was. What was touching her face? She wiped at it again frantically. Her hand came away wet. "Rain!" she said out loud, as a flash of lightning illuminated the old barn and she remembered where she was.

"Wake up, kids," Jake said at the same time. "It's fixing to storm!"

"Grab your stuff, and let's get into the barn," Leigh said. "Amanda, hurry up! Don't just sit there. Do you want to get struck by lightning?"

Amanda wrapped her sleeping bag around her and began stumbling groggily in the wrong direction. Leigh turned her around and gave her a push toward the barn.

Megan and the others gathered up their sleeping bags as fast as they could and followed Jake into the barn. The wind had been blowing fiercely outside, but the air was quiet and still inside the huge building. Standing just inside the door, they all looked out at the stormy pasture and woods. Lightning flashed for several seconds; then, with a huge clap of thunder, rain began to pour down.

"Whew. We made it inside just in time," Leigh said.

"You're not kidding," Jake said. "It's raining buckets."

Rain was blowing in the door now. They stepped back to keep from getting wet. Lightning showed them the inside of the barn every few seconds, blinding them with its brightness, then left them in total darkness.

"It sure is dark in here," Megan said, huddling next to Chloe.

"You're standing on my foot." Keith's voice came from behind Megan.

"Sorry," Megan said. "I thought you were Chloe."

"I'm right here, Meg," Chloe said.

Megan groped her way to her and took her friend's arm. "Boy, I'd sure hate to be out here all alone," she said.

"Shoot," Jake said.

"What's the matter?" Leigh asked.

"I brought a flashlight, but it's in the truck," he explained.

"Are you going to get it?" Megan wanted to know.

"Not till this rain slows down a little," Jake said. "I reckon we'll just have to tough it out in the dark. At least it's dry in here."

"What about the horses?" Max asked.

"They'll just have to tough it out, too," Jake said.

"Couldn't we let them in here with us?" Chloe asked. "I feel so sorry for them out in the storm."

"It won't hurt them," Leigh said. "Remember, horses in the wild live outside in all kinds of weather. They'll be all right."

They put their sleeping bags down away from the windows so they wouldn't get wet. Then they lay down again and listened to the storm raging outside. Megan tried not to think about what might be lurking in the shadowy corners of the old barn.

She must have drifted off again, because suddenly she was opening her eyes. The rain was still coming steadily down. She realized that the others must have fallen asleep, too, because everyone was quiet.

Megan had a strange feeling in the pit of her stomach, and she felt tense, as if she were expecting something to happen. Lightning flashed again. In the brief glare, Megan saw something in the far corner of the barn. She felt her heart start to pound as she sat up, instantly alert. She peered into the blackness, waiting for the next flash of lightning. Then it came. A huge, crackling bolt of lightning ripped through the air, answered by a deafening boom of thunder. In the corner of the barn, Megan saw it: the figure of a girl in a long white dress!

The girl's arms were outstretched, and her face looked anguished, as if she were trying to move or speak and was somehow unable to. She cried out, a low, eerie, moaning sound. In the next flash of lightning, the girl vanished!

Megan had been unable to utter a sound when she saw the figure of the girl. Now she found her voice. She screamed as long and loud as she ever had. She could have sworn she heard an answering scream coming from the corner where the girl had disappeared. A huge gust of wind whipped through the barn, followed by a loud thud from the corner. Thunder clapped angrily overhead.

"What's wrong?" Jake was on his feet in an instant. "Who's screaming? What's the matter?"

"Jake, I saw her again!" Megan said. "I saw the ghost! The ghost of the girl from the plantation, just like you told us! I saw her, I saw her—I swear! She was right there in the corner, and then she just disappeared. And, Jake"—Megan gulped in fear— "she made a noise, a terrible noise. Like moaning and crying . . ." Megan could hardly breathe, she was so frightened.

Leigh put an arm around her and rubbed her back soothingly. "Megan, you were dreaming. You were just having a bad dream, honey. There's no ghost. There's just us."

"No!" Megan insisted. "I *saw* her. She was *right there.*" Megan pointed at the empty corner as lightning blinked again.

"Did anybody else see anything?" Jake asked.

Nobody had.

"I never should have let y'all tell all those spooky stories," Jake said. "Okay, the storm's about over now. Let's all just try and get some sleep. It'll be daylight in a few hours." He lay down, muttering something about letting himself get talked into camping out with a bunch of kids.

"I wasn't dreaming," Megan said quietly. "I saw it. It was there, and then it disappeared."

"Go to sleep, Megan," Max said.

Somehow, they all did go to sleep again. When

they woke up in the morning, the sky was clear and cloudless. The wet grass and the leaves and branches that had blown down were the only signs left of the fierce storm. A long rectangle of sunlight crept across the old wooden floor, showing them the inside of the barn for the first time.

Megan slowly sat up and looked around her. There were six stalls along the left side of the barn. A rickety old ladder led to a hayloft overhead. The loft came halfway across the length of the barn and then stopped. Hanging all over the walls along the right side were old tools, bridles, and harnesses.

"Wow," Keith said as he rolled up his sleeping bag. "Just look at all this neat old stuff."

"Cool," Max said, stretching his arms over his head. "Look at that old bridle. It looks like someone made the bit themselves."

"Someone did," Jake said. "Back then, the black-smith didn't just make shoes for horses. He made all kinds of tools and things. I'm going outside to check on the horses. Y'all get your stuff together and start loading it up in the back of my truck."

In a minute, Jake appeared by the truck. He looked annoyed. Soon they found out why. "That dad-gum horse of Amanda's is gone again. He must have jumped out of the paddock in the night." Jake shook his head. "That horse is nothing but trouble. Amanda, you'll just have to ride back with me in the truck." Jake looked around. "Where is Amanda?" he asked.

"I haven't seen her," Megan said, dumping her sleeping bag into the bed of the truck.

"Me neither," Chloe said.

"Keith, Max, is Amanda in the barn with you?" Leigh called.

"No," they shouted.

"Now, where could she be?" Jake said.

9

"AMANDA," THE CHILDREN CALLED.

"Amanda, where are you?" Jake's voice echoed in the morning quiet. There was no reply. Megan and the other campers looked all over for the missing girl. All they found was her sleeping bag and her robe and slippers on the floor of the barn. Megan put them in the back of the truck.

Jake came out of the woods, shaking his head. "Now, where could that kid have gone?"

"Maybe she went back to the barn," Keith suggested.

"But why would she go all alone?" Leigh asked.

"Maybe she took Prince," Megan said. "They're both gone."

"But his tack's still here. She couldn't ride him without it," Leigh pointed out.

"Maybe she rode him bareback. He was wearing his halter," Max said.

"Amanda? I doubt it," Leigh said. "She has enough trouble riding that horse with all his tack. I can't see her getting on him bareback and riding back to the barn all alone. Are you sure none of you saw her this morning?" Leigh was starting to sound worried.

"I didn't see her at all," Megan said.

"None of us did," Max said.

"Max, are you sure she's not in the old barn?" Leigh said.

"I'm sure she wasn't in there before, but we can go look again," Max offered. The group walked through the barn one more time, but there was no sign of Amanda. Jake even boosted Keith up so he could look in the hayloft, but there was nothing there except dust and straw and a few old burlap sacks.

"Well," Jake said, "she's sure not here. Why don't we head on back to the main barn. Maybe we'll find her along the way."

They tacked up the horses and headed back. When they got to the barn, the horses went eagerly to their grain buckets and began to eat. There was a big box of doughnuts waiting for the campers. Jake went to the office to see if Amanda had shown up, while the four children sat at the picnic table munching doughnuts and talking about their exciting night.

"I know I wasn't dreaming," Megan insisted. "She was wearing a long white dress just like they used to wear in the old days. Her arms were stretched out, and she looked like she was trying to tell me something. Then, when she disappeared, there was this big gust of wind and a loud bang!"

"So how come you're the only one who saw her?" Max said, helping himself to a second doughnut. "Remember what Leigh said? People believe what they want to believe. Probably what you saw was just some of that old junk in the barn, and in the lightning it looked like something else."

"No," Megan said firmly. "It was her. It was the ghost. And I know she was trying to tell me something." Megan jumped off the picnic table.

"Where are you going, Meg?" Chloe asked.

"I'm going to see if anybody claimed the locket. I'll bet you anything there's some reason why that deer led me to it. There must be."

"Animals have ways of telling people things," Chloe said. "Once, my dog Jenny wouldn't go into the carport, and you know what? My dad found a big old rattlesnake in there."

"See?" Megan said. "I bet the deer *was* trying to tell me something." Megan marched off toward the office.

She was about to push open the screen door when she heard Jake and Sharon talking inside. Megan reached out to knock on the door, but something about the tone of their voices stopped her. Instead, she stood where she was, just outside the door, and listened.

"Are you sure she wasn't just around there someplace and didn't hear you leaving?" Sharon was saying.

"Sharon, I looked all over the place for her. We all did. There's no way she could've been anywhere near there and not heard us calling her. Are her parents sure she's not at home?" Jake sounded worried.

"They're looking right now, in case she came home alone and just didn't let them know she was there. But, Jake, you know it's not likely she'd do that. Amanda's used to being driven around in a limo; I doubt she could even give directions to her home, much less get herself there before eight o'clock in the morning. Besides, all her things were still in your truck." Sharon's voice grew lower and even more urgent. "Jake, I'm afraid something bad may have happened to Amanda."

"I'm going back up to the old barn to have another look around," Jake said. "I've got the portable phone. Call me on the other line as soon as you hear anything from the Sloanes. And don't let the other kids get wind of this until we know what we're dealing with. I don't want to scare them." His voice got closer to the door as he spoke. Megan quickly stepped forward and knocked on the door, so that Jake and Sharon wouldn't know she had been listening to their conversation. "Megan," Jake said, looking surprised to see her. "What do you need?"

"Is Sharon in there?" Megan asked. "I want to ask her something."

"Come in, Megan," Sharon said. "What is it?"

Jake held the door for Megan, then left. Megan stepped up to Sharon's desk and said, "I was wondering if anybody had claimed the locket I turned in to the lost-and-found. It's been about a week, and Jake said I could keep it if nobody claimed it by that time. Remember?"

Sharon pulled open her desk drawer and took out the locket. "I guess you might as well have it. If anybody comes looking for it, you might have to give it back, though. Here you go." Sharon held out the locket to Megan.

"Thank you," Megan said, slipping the locket around her neck.

Then the phone rang. Sharon answered it quickly: "Thistle Ridge Farm."

Megan saw a look of concern flash across Sharon's face for a moment before her expression became neutral.

"Just a minute," she said into the phone. "Megan, would you excuse me, please?"

Megan nodded and hurried out. As the screen door closed behind her, she hear Sharon say into the phone, "Then she hasn't turned up yet?"

Megan went back to the courtyard.

"Did you get the locket?" Chloe asked.

"Right here." She gestured at the necklace, but her mind was on something else. "You guys," she said breathlessly. "Guess what?" Quickly, she told them what she'd overheard in the office. "And

Amanda's not at home, either," she finished. "Her parents called just as I was leaving."

"Oh, no," Chloe looked stricken. "What if she's been hurt?"

"Her parents are rich. What if she's been kidnapped?" Keith said. They all looked at each other for a moment in complete silence.

"Maybe she's just lost," Max finally said. "Maybe she went out in the storm last night and just got turned around and couldn't find her way back."

"That sounds like Amanda," Keith agreed. "Maybe we should go look for her."

"Sharon and Jake sounded really worried," Megan said. "Wouldn't it be great if we found her before they end up calling the police or something?"

"Maybe if we go back to the pasture and look around, we'll find a clue that'll tell us where she might be," Keith said.

"Thistle Ridge Detectives!" Megan grinned at them. The four of them high-fived each other. "Let's go!"

"Megan, wait," Max said. "Remember what Sharon said about going off on our own without telling anyone? I don't want to get in trouble."

They all hesitated. Then Megan remembered something. "She said we had to tell someone where we were going during *camp*. This is Saturday; there is no camp today."

"I still think we should tell someone where we're going," Max said.

"If we tell them, they're not going to let us go.

They'll be afraid that something will happen to us, too," Megan said.

"She's right," Keith said. "Let's just go. We all have our own horses."

"Except for me," Chloe said. "I can't take Peeps without asking first."

They all thought for a moment. "I know," Keith said. "You can ride double with me. Penny can carry us both. My sister and I used to ride her together all the time."

"Are you sure?" Chloe sounded doubtful. "How will we both fit in the saddle?"

"We'll go bareback," Keith said.

"Yeah, let's all go bareback!" Megan said. "That way, we can get out of the barn quicker."

"All right," Chloe said, still looking a little worried.

"We'll have to sneak out one at a time," Megan said, "so we don't attract attention. Everybody meet in ten minutes, down by the tree that got struck by lightning."

"Right. Max and I will go down first, so if anybody sees us, they'll just think that we're going to turn out Penny and Popsicle," Keith said.

"Okay," Max said. "Let's go."

They all made it down to the dead tree without anybody questioning them, or even seeming to notice. Megan was the only one who could mount up bareback without help, so she had to give everyone else a leg up. "Score another one for the ponies," she said, scrambling up on Pixie's dark, dappled back without any trouble at all. She had tied an extra lead line around her waist, in case they saw Prince Charming.

They decided to go in different directions, so they could cover more ground. "Everybody cover your territory, and then meet back here in about half an hour. And watch out for Jake!" Megan reminded them.

Max went toward the lake. Chloe put her arms around Keith's waist as he jogged Penny toward the creek that bounded Thistle Ridge's acres on the south side. Megan headed Pixie toward the back pasture, where they'd been playing hide-and-seek.

She had just come to the tree that they used as the base when she saw something light-colored move through the woods. "Amanda?" she called. There was no answer. She trotted toward the edge of the woods and peered in, trying to see what had moved there. A narrow path wound through the trees. Pixie's ears were pricked forward alertly and Megan felt the pony's body grow tense as they trotted down the path. She felt a little nervous herself. She shortened the reins and wished she had put Pixie's saddle on after all.

She soon discovered why Pixie was acting so jumpy. They had come upon a doe and her fawn, lying hidden in the thick brush near the edge of the path. The doe quickly got to her feet and stood quivering, her large eyes filled with fear and indecision. Megan was sure it was the same deer that had led her to the pile of stones where she'd found the locket.

Pixie stood with her front legs spread apart as if she were ready to run in any direction. The fawn lay curled up in the brush, its eyes half closed. It shook its head sleepily and blinked, as if trying to stay awake. Tentatively, Pixie put out her nose and sniffed at the baby deer. The fawn laid its little head back down and closed its eyes. Hoping the deer wouldn't move suddenly. Megan sat still, barely breathing. She still didn't know if Pixie would spook and bolt.

Megan then noticed that the mother deer seemed to relax. The doe lowered her head and began to nibble at some leaves. Pixie gave a gentle snort and seemed to calm down, too. Megan sighed with relief. She hadn't even realized she'd been holding her breath. She guessed Pixie was finally getting used to the deer.

Megan was just about to move on when there was a sound in the trees behind them. Pixie's head shot up. So did the doe's. Megan just had time to gather up the reins as she looked over her shoulder and saw Prince Charming crashing through the brush toward them.

The doe bleated to her fawn, who jumped to its spindly legs. They took off down the path. Pixie took off after them. Megan turned to see Prince Charming headed after her and Pixie, frightening the pony more as he galloped up on her tail. Megan wrapped her legs around Pixie and held on as best she could as they tore through the brush.

The two deer had run up the path ahead of them. Now they veered off to one side. Pixie followed them into the woods to the side of the trail, almost unseating Megan. Somehow, she managed to stay on but then found herself unable to sit up to stop Pixie. The tree branches were thick and low, so she had to keep her head down almost below Pixie's neck to keep from getting swiped off by a branch. She grabbed mane and gritted her teeth, determined to stay on until they were clear of the trees.

A little way ahead, she thought she saw a patch of sun through the thick trees. She lost sight of the two deer, who had somehow vanished into the brush. A branch scraped across her face just then, forcing her to close her eyes. When she opened them, she expected to see a clearing where she could sit up and stop Pixie. Instead, when she opened her eyes, she realized she was cantering toward a stone wall!

To the right and left were thick trees and brush. There was no way to turn around, and Megan couldn't stop. Prince Charming's hooves were thundering behind her. Megan had just enough time to grab mane before Pixie rocked back on her haunches and sailed over the stone wall! She landed on the other side and stopped abruptly.

Megan sat panting on Pixie's back. She could hardly believe she was still on her pony. For a second, she felt relieved that the worst was over. Then she looked around her, wondering why she'd come across a stone wall in the middle of the woods. The wall was almost four feet high, except in places where it had begun to crumble. It enclosed an area about the size of four big box stalls. Suddenly, Megan realized where she was. She gasped and shuddered, feeling a chill run through her. She and Pixie had just jumped into *a graveyard!*

10

Around Megan were several old tombstones, some plain, some with fancy carvings. On top of one was a large statue of an angel. Most of the stones were covered with moss or darkened with age, so that it was difficult to make out the lettering on them.

Slowly, Megan slid off Pixie and stood leaning against the pony's shoulder, trying to catch her breath. She had managed to put the scare from the night before out of her head for most of the day, but now she remembered the figure in white, and Jake's ghost story. She felt her heart begin to pound all over again. To reassure herself, she began to say to herself over and over, "There's no such thing as ghosts, there's no such thing as ghosts, there's no such thing as . . ."

The words died on her lips as she gazed at the

statue of the angel. She had the feeling it was watching her. She could have sworn the angel's eyes had moved in the pale marble face. Then she read the inscription at the base of the statue. The engraved letters had weathered away in places, but she was able to make out most of it.

" 'Marley Kathryn Dellbrook,' " she read aloud. " 'Born December 20, 1840 . . . Died January 22, 1852 . . . Our little angel rides in heaven.' " Megan looked up at the statue and realized that the angel was riding a horse.

"She was just eleven," Megan murmured. "Exactly my age. December 20 . . . that's *my* birthday!" Megan put her hand to her throat and felt the chain around her neck. Suddenly, she remembered the locket!

She pulled it out and looked at it again, trying to read the initials. " 'M. K. . . .' " she read aloud. The third initial was still tarnished and difficult to make out. She rubbed and polished it with her shirttail, until at last it began to come clean, and she could make it out. " 'M. K. D.,' " she whispered. She stared at the engraving on the angel statue. " 'Marley Kathryn Dellbrook—M. K. D.' " Megan gulped as she realized the truth. *"The locket belonged to the girl in the fire."*

It was so silent in the little cemetery that when a stick snapped loudly in the brush behind her, Megan almost jumped out of her skin. Pixie started, too, and let out a snort. Then there came an answering snort from the other side of the wall, and a big white head peered over it. Megan was relieved to see that it was only Prince Charming.

Then she remembered why she'd come out to the pasture in the first place. She hadn't found any clues to Amanda's whereabouts, but she had at least found Prince Charming. She decided to try to catch him before she met the others back at the old tree.

But how was she going to get out of the graveyard? Strangely, there was no gate in the wall. There was a stile—rotting wooden steps just wide enough for a person to walk upon led up to and over the wall. But they didn't look safe, and Pixie could never walk over them anyway. Megan couldn't just leave her pony. She didn't like the idea, but the only way out that she could see was to jump back over the wall.

Having made up her mind, she chose to jump over to the lowest section of the wall, which happened to be near the stile. She circled Pixie toward the farthest corner from it, to get an approach. Picking up a trot, she headed for the wall. She had to swerve a little in the approach to avoid one of the headstones. As she trotted closer to the wall, she bent forward into two-point position and prepared for the jump. To her surprise, right at the base of the wall, Pixie stopped. Megan was thrown onto Pixie's neck, but luckily she had grabbed mane and managed to stay on. She pushed herself back into position, picked up the reins, and circled

Pixie, preparing to come at it again. "Come on, Pixie, you can do it," she urged.

This time, she gave Pixie a good kick and made a clucking sound to encourage her as they got to the base of the wall. But, again, Pixie refused to jump. Megan ended up on Pixie's shoulders again, grabbing neck to stay on. Again she managed to push herself back onto Pixie's back. Megan was puzzled. It just wasn't like Pixie to refuse.

A sudden chill gripped Megan, and she realized she was shivering. She was sure she felt a cold draft of air coming from the ground near the base of the wall. Megan looked more closely and saw that there was an opening under the steps. She began to feel afraid again. Was it an open grave? Was that why Pixie wouldn't jump the wall near the opening?

She looked around for another place to jump the wall, but there just wasn't a good approach to any of the lower sections; everywhere she looked, gravestones blocked her path. She began to feel panicked. Was she trapped in this cemetery? She could get off and climb over the wall, but how could she leave her pony? She didn't know what to do. Then she heard a noise that made her skin turn to ice. An eery wailing sound was coming from the opening under the steps.

Megan was petrified as she listened to the mournful crying sound. She wanted to cry herself, but her throat was blocked with a huge lump of fear.

Megan had just begun to wonder if a person could actually die of fright, when she heard Prince Charming moving in the bushes outside the wall. His footsteps seemed to be moving away from her. Suddenly, he seemed to her like the only friendly thing within miles. With great effort, she found her voice.

"Prince!" she managed to croak. "Here, boy!" She clucked at him, then pleaded, her voice breaking. "Please don't leave us!"

For a moment, there was silence. Then she heard his footsteps approaching again. She recognized the three-beat sound of his canter coming closer and closer to the other side of the wall. Suddenly, she saw his head and shoulders and then the rest of his body come sailing over the wall. He had jumped into the graveyard!

Megan never thought she'd be so glad to see Amanda's troublesome horse. He trotted up to Pixie, and they sniffed at each other, blowing air into each other's nostrils. Then Prince trotted once around the perimeter of the graveyard, avoiding the area near the steps where Pixie had refused to jump. Next, Prince stopped and stood looking at them. He whinnied and began trotting around the edge of the graveyard again. *Follow me*, his expression seemed to say.

Once more, he trotted around the little cemetery. Then the white horse turned and cantered straight at the wall where he'd jumped into the cemetery. Megan realized that he was going to jump out again. She knew that the herd instinct in horses is strong and that one horse will often do what he sees another horse do. She quickly squeezed Pixie's sides and sent her cantering on Prince's heels, hoping the pony would jump out of the cemetery after him.

Prince Charming sailed easily over the stone wall. Pixie sprang into the air after him, tucking her knees up to her chin as she neatly cleared the fence. Megan braced herself for the landing on the other side and managed not to slip off.

"Whew!" she said with relief. Prince Charming began to trot away. Pixie trotted off after him. Megan let her go, glad to be out of the scary graveyard and anxious to get as far away from it as she could. But before she get too far, she thought she heard the ghostly wailing sound coming from the other side of the wall. It gave her goose bumps, and she urged Pixie to go faster.

Pixie followed Prince along the crest of the ridge, and soon they came into a clearing. Megan recognized the old barn before her. "Oh, no, not again," she said to herself. Megan was pretty sure she'd had enough scary experiences lately to last the rest of her life. To her dismay, Prince Charming trotted right into the old barn.

"I guess we have to go in after him, Pixie." Taking a big breath, Megan trotted up to the barn, dismounted, and led Pixie in.

Just inside, Megan paused and looked around fearfully, half expecting to see the ghost again. She was glad Prince and Pixie were with her, even if they were only animals. The big barn appeared the same inside as it had that morning. Megan looked at the old tools and harnesses hanging on the walls. Sunlight leaked through the kudzu-covered windows over each stall, casting mottled shadows on the dusty wooden floor.

Prince had gone into the last stall at the end of the barn. He stood with his head sticking out the open door of the stall and looked at Megan as if he still expected her to follow him. Megan realized that all she had to do was close the stall door and she would have him captured. She led Pixie slowly toward the end of the barn, then pushed Prince back and closed the door of the stall.

The latch on the door was old and stiff and refused to slide. Megan pushed at it as hard as she could, but it wouldn't budge. Frustrated, she looked around for something to hit it with and spied an old mallet hanging on the wall near the top of the ladder that led to the loft. She stuck Pixie in the stall next to Prince Charming, though the latch on that stall wouldn't close, either. She left them anyway, hoping they wouldn't escape before she returned, and went after the mallet.

It was too high to reach without climbing the ladder. Gingerly, she stepped on the first rung and paused, testing it to see if it would hold her weight. When it did, she took another step up. When she was far enough up the ladder, she peered over the edge of the loft. It was mostly empty, as Keith had said, except for some old straw and a dusty pile of burlap sacks.

Megan climbed up one more step and wrapped one arm around a support post that ran from floor to ceiling at the edge of the loft. Then she leaned slowly out toward the wall where the mallet was hanging. Her fingertips were touching it, but she couldn't quite grasp it. She made a quick swipe at it and managed to knock it down from the wall. At the same time, she felt the old rung of the ladder give way under her feet!

She slipped and would have fallen if she hadn't been hanging on to the post. She grabbed at it with her other arm and hung on, wincing as she felt splinters jabbing into her arms. She came to rest with her arms around the post, her elbows propped on the edge of the loft and her feet dangling in the air ten feet above the floor of the barn.

Hugging the post, she managed to bring one leg up far enough to get her foot over the edge of the loft. She paused for a moment, gathering up her strength. Then, with all her might, she pulled herself up toward the edge and scrambled over, landing on the dusty floor of the loft.

For a moment she lay with her eyes closed, grateful for the solid feel of the floorboards under her back. Then the stinging pain of the splinters made her wince again, and she opened her eyes and sat up. Both arms were badly scraped and full of splinters from the rough post. There was an ugly scratch all along her left side that was beginning to bleed.

Her left arm had been badly wrenched as well. It felt strained and throbbed dully. She knew she was lucky she hadn't fallen and been hurt even worse.

Megan pulled out the splinters as best she could and then got slowly to her feet. She felt a little shaky, but at least her legs worked fine. She began searching the corners of the left, looking for a rope or a ladder or anything she could use to get herself down.

At the far end of the loft was a window. She knelt and looked out. There was a beautiful view of the back pasture and the land beyond. Storm clouds were piling up once again in the southwestern sky. Megan knew they probably meant another afternoon thundershower. She sat down cross-legged and gazed out at the landscape as she tried to think of a way to get down.

Then she saw Prince Charming go trotting by underneath the window. Pixie was right behind him. "Shoot!" Megan said out loud. "They must've figured out the doors weren't latched." She felt her heart sink as the two horses trotted around the corner of the barn out of sight. Now she was all alone in the old barn.

She felt panic creeping up from her stomach and into her heart. She pushed it down. "Silly!" she told herself firmly. "Be brave. Max and Chloe and Keith know I'm out here somewhere. They'll come looking for me when I don't meet them at the tree . . . I hope."

She looked away from the window and saw

something sticking out from a crevice under the sill. Curious, she slid her hand under and pulled out a little book, bound in blue leather and held closed with a tiny lock. "What's this?" she said to herself, forgetting her fear.

She turned the little book over and brushed off the dust. There weren't any markings on the cover. She tried to open it, but the little latch was locked or jammed. Then she remembered the key in the locket. Quickly, she took it out and tried it in the little lock. It slid in and turned easily. With a tiny click, the latch sprang open.

The pages inside were covered with handwriting in scratchy blue ink. Some of the writing was very clear and easy to read, while on other pages water must have seeped in and blurred the ink. The pages in the beginning of the journal were written in a childish scrawl, while the pages toward the end were covered with line after line of elegant penmanship. Megan turned back to the first page and read, " 'Marley Kathryn Dellbrook. My journal. Christmas Day, 1849.' "

Megan could hardly believe it. First she had found the locket, then the graveyard, and now Marley's journal. She had the distinct feeling that she was about to discover something important about the girl who had lived more than a century ago. She turned the brittle page and began to read out loud.

11

" 'I BEGIN THIS JOURNAL CHRISTMAS NIGHT, 1849. Mother gave it to me, and a beautiful silver locket, engraved with my initials and set with a diamond, and with a picture of her inside.' "

Megan gazed at the locket again, then opened it and studied the portrait of the woman inside—Marley's mother. She peered into the woman's dark eyes, wondering if Marley had looked anything like her mother. Megan would have given anything to look like her own mother. She touched her cheek, glad that at least she had inherited her mom's deep dimples. Then she read on.

" 'But Papa gave me the best gift of all. First, they made me put on shoes and wear my wrap right over my gown. Then they tied a cloth over my eyes to blindfold me and directly I was led down to the pasture fence. When I uncovered my eyes, there was Isaac, our stableboy, holding the most beautiful white pony! And he's to be mine, and I'm to ride out with Papa every day! I made Isaac set me up on him straightaway and lead me about the paddock. I wanted to go on my own, but Papa says I must first let Old Henry give me lessons. I don't know what for. I know I can ride him. I'm going to call him Nugget, because he's good as gold. I can't wait till I get on him again! This must be the happiest Christmas that ever there was!' "

Megan turned the page and read further.

" 'January 1st, 1850. Today I was allowed out on Nugget with the New Year's Day Hunt. Old Henry kept me on a lead beside him. I must say it was tiring, and once I fell off, but I had a grand time, and in the end they let me jump over the little coop in the North pasture.' "

Megan looked out the window at the rolling hills and imagined going fox hunting with all the ladies and gentlemen in their fancy attire. She could almost hear the bugle call and the hounds baying. She hoped one day she could try it.

The next entries were all about Marley's lessons on Nugget and her life on the plantation. Megan learned that Marley had a tutor, and a slave girl named Mary Ann to dress her and look after her. Mary Ann was just twelve at the time Marley wrote about her. Megan thought it was strange that a twelve-year-old girl would have to be responsible for another child.

Megan had to skip over a large section of the

journal that had somehow gotten wet. The next entry that she could read was dated March 1851 and described the new overseer that Marley's father had hired. Megan could tell from Marley's description that she didn't think much of him. "Mr. Latimer, the new overseer, met us as I rode out with Papa this evening,'" Megan read. "'He made much of the fact that I was riding astride, and not side-saddle as ladies are supposed to do. I said that whenever a lady falls off, they say it's because she's a poor rider, and when a man falls off, he's called a brave equestrian. So I intended to fall off like a man, if ever I did. Mr. Latimer laughed at me and said Papa ought to send me in to my needlework or I'd make too spirited a wench to be any man's wife. I feel sorry for whoever may become Mr. Latimer's wife. I don't want to be any man's wife; I want to ride horses all my life. One day I'll inherit this plantation. When I do, I'll make sure the first thing I do is excuse Mr. Latimer from his post. And I'll never sell the slaves away from their families.'"

In a later entry, Marley told how Mr. Latimer had sold Mary Ann away from the plantation and her family, simply because he didn't like how she'd answered him once. This page was spotted with dried droplets. Megan wondered if they were tears.

The next legible entry began, "July 7th, 1851." Megan read, "'I go down to the pasture fence each night before bedtime to pat Nugget and feed him lumps of sugar. If I climb upon the fence, that is the signal that Mr. Latimer is in the main house with

117

Papa and the coast is clear for the slaves. Then they may pass safely from the slave quarters to the barn and make their escape. But if I stand on the ground and only look out at the pasture, or if I am not there at all, they know that Mr. Latimer is about the property with his dogs, and they must beware.' "

There was another section of pages too blurred to make out, then Megan read, " 'Mother and I helped Martha, Jacob, and Little Alice out tonight. Peter and Isaac have already made it out safely. Papa and Mr. Latimer are beside themselves wondering how they keep losing slaves in spite of the patrollers and the extra measures they have taken to prevent their escaping. I wonder, if Papa knew that Mother and I have been helping their cause, would he send me south on the chain gang as he did to my Mary Ann, or have me beaten senseless as he did to Peter the day he caught him poaching? So far, no one has figured out our secret. Peter and Isaac were clever to build the cemetery wall with a stile, rather than a gate, so that the end of the passage is invisible. They told Papa it was to keep out the animals that might bother the graves. No one suspected that all the while they were digging Uncle Ezra's grave by day, by night they were digging the tunnel. I am sitting now in Nugget's stall, directly over the trapdoor. Old Henry keeps the bedding deep; Nugget stands by peacefully eating his grain. Who would guess that underneath us is the entrance to the secret tunnel, by which we are

118

helping the slaves to make their way north toward
Pennsylvania and Freedom?' "

Megan looked up. "Trapdoor?" she mused. "Tunnel?" Abruptly, she put down the book and crawled
toward the corner of the loft. She brushed away
the straw from a section of floor, sneezing as she
waited for the dust to settle. Then she lay on her
stomach and peered through a crack in the
floorboards.

She was directly over the last stall in the corner.
In a second, she saw what she was looking for.
Barely visible in the floor of the stall was the out-
line of a trapdoor. Slowly, a little smile crossed
her face.

The last entry was dated January 1852. " 'It has
been raining every day for two weeks. The lake is
over the levy, and Old Henry told me the bridge
over the creek has washed out. The tunnel floods
easily, as it is so close to the well. Last week, three
were drowned in it; they had to stay hidden as Mr.
Latimer chose that night to search the woods all
about the cemetery while it rained and rained. Not
knowing how to swim, they were trapped as the
water filled the tunnel. All escape plans are off until
the rain stops and the water goes down. . . .' " The
rest of the entry was a blur, as were the last few
pages of the journal. Megan closed the little book.

"She was so much like me," she said to herself,
thinking of Marley. Then she realized that the light
in the barn had become even dimmer. The air was
thick and still. Suddenly, there was a flash of light-

ning, followed by a rumble of thunder. Megan looked uneasily around the barn. She shuddered, remembering the terrifying ghostly figure she had seen the night before. Lightning cracked again, lighting up the corner where the trapdoor lay in the floor. Megan remembered how the ghost had stood right over that spot before it had vanished with a gust of wind and a loud bang. Suddenly she jumped to her feet.

"Ghost!" she exclaimed. "That was no ghost!" She couldn't help grinning as she realized what she had seen. "That was Amanda!"

The first drops of rain hit the tin roof of the barn with a patter. Megan knew she had to move fast. She began searching the loft for anything she might use to get herself down. A gust of wind blew in the open window, and there was a squeaking sound from overhead. Megan looked up and saw a rope hanging from a pulley fastened to one of the broad cross-beams that supported the roof. It was just above her head. She jumped at it twice, trying to reach it, and at last caught hold of it. She pulled the rope down and examined it. It looked old and dry. The end was frayed, as if it had broken once before.

"It'll just have to hold me," Megan said. Quickly, she tied a thick knot in the end of the rope. She sat down with her legs hanging over the edge of the loft and took the other end of the rope in her hands. She took a deep breath, wrapped her legs securely around the knot, and slowly slid off the edge.

She felt her sore arm ache as she swung slightly in the air and heard the rope stretch and groan with her weight. The pulley creaked overhead, but it held. Slowly, she began to let herself down, wincing each time she had to use her left arm. In a few seconds, she felt her feet touch the ground, and she was safe.

Megan ran to the corner stall and tried to lift the trapdoor, but it fit tightly around the edges. She couldn't see a handle or a lock anywhere.

She ran out of the barn and headed for the old graveyard as fast as she could. The rain was coming down hard now. Lightning flashed all around her as she tore down the path, ducking branches and pushing aside bushes. She came around a turn and almost ran into the cemetery wall. She ran around it, looking for the steps that led over it. When she found them, she saw that the steps had long ago rotted and collapsed, just as she'd feared. The wall was as high as Megan's head in most places. The stones were smooth, so that there were no holds where she might climb over.

Then she heard the same "ghostly" wailing she had heard with Pixie, only it was growing louder as the rain came down harder and the thunder rolled. Megan thought about going for help, but she realized that there might not be time. The tunnel must already have water in it from the storm the night before. It might not be much longer before it flooded completely.

Megan jumped at the wall and felt her fingers catch over the top. Her feet scrabbled at the wall, sliding uselessly on the slippery stones. Pain shot through her side, and she had to let go. She looked around for a tree she might climb, but there were none that she could see with branches low enough. She was about to run for the main barn for help when suddenly Prince Charming appeared in the trees.

"Prince!" Megan said. "Here, boy." She pulled up a handful of greenery and offered it to him. The friendly, nosy horse came toward her willingly and gobbled the leaves from her outstretched hand. She caught him by his halter and quickly undid the lead line that was still around her waist.

She clipped it to the halter on one side and tied the other end to form makeshift reins. Then she grabbed a handful of mane, counted to three, and managed to vault herself onto Prince's back. "Wow," she said, patting him. "You're tall."

Clinging to the powerful horse, she trotted him away from the cemetery. Then she pulled up and turned to face the wall. "Okay, Prince. Time to rescue Amanda." She thumped him with her legs and felt him canter in an easy, loping stride that carried them toward the wall. She held her breath, half afraid he would refuse. But in the next instant, she went sailing over the wall on the big white horse. As soon as they landed, she slid off and ran to the old, rotten steps where she'd seen the opening in the stones.

The crying was loud and frantic now. Megan could hear rushing water even over the sound of the rain. She began pulling loose stones away from the opening and had soon exposed a hole big enough for someone her size to fit through. She stuck her head into the opening and looked around, but she couldn't see anything.

"Amanda?" she yelled. The sound of the water inside the hole was loud. "Amanda! Are you in there? Can you hear me?"

The wailing had stopped. "Megan?" said a voice that could only be Amanda's.

"Yes, it's me! Are you okay?"

A very dirty face appeared below her. It was Amanda, looking very scared and soaking wet, still in her nightgown from the campout. Megan felt sorry for her, but for a second she enjoyed seeing Amanda—who was always criticizing Chloe for looking dirty—in her filthy, sodden gown.

"Megan, the water is up to my waist, and it's getting higher every minute! Please, get me out of here!" Amanda sobbed. "And hurry!"

"I'm going to," Megan said determinedly. She stuck out her hand. "Here, can you reach me?"

Amanda reached up, but she was a foot short of reaching Megan's hand. "Megan, please help me!" Amanda begged.

"I'm going to, I promise. Just hold on!"

Megan ran to Prince Charming and untied the

lead line from his halter. Then she lowered one end of it into the hole. Amanda reached it easily. Megan tried hard to pull her up with the lead line, ignoring the sharp pain in her side and arm, but it was no use. Amanda was a year older than Megan and outweighed her by several pounds. Megan simply couldn't lift her.

The water was now up to Amanda's chest, and still rising. Megan began to feel frightened that she would be unable to get Amanda out in time. What should she do? She was afraid to leave her and go for help. She thought about climbing down into the tunnel and trying to boost her out, but she wasn't sure she could. And she doubted even more that Amanda would be able to pull her out. Then she had an idea.

"Amanda, let go of the lead line for a minute," she instructed her.

"What are you going to do? Don't leave me, Megan, please? I'll do anything you say. Just please get me out of here!" Amanda cried.

Megan caught Prince Charming again and clipped the lead line to his halter. Then she passed the other end down to Amanda. The water was almost up to her neck now.

"Take the lead line and tie it around your waist," Megan instructed. "Make sure you tie a good knot." Amanda did as she was told.

"Okay, now hold on tight," Megan said. She began to back Prince away from the tunnel. As she had hoped, as soon as he figured out he was tied to something, he jerked his head up and began to back up furiously. Amanda was lifted to the opening of the tunnel, where she was able to heave herself up onto the ground.

Megan quickly unclipped the lead line so that Amanda wouldn't be dragged and held Prince by the halter, patting him soothingly. "Good boy," she said to him. He snorted and shoved at her with his nose, almost knocking her down. Megan laughed.

"What's so funny?" Amanda said indignantly.

"Nothing," Megan said. "Amanda, untie the lead line. We've got to get back to the barn. Everyone will be worried by now. Especially with both of us missing."

Megan tied the lead line onto Prince's halter again and gave Amanda a leg up. Then she led Prince over to a gravestone and used it as a mounting block to get herself on in front of Amanda. "Okay, hold on tight," Megan said to Amanda. "And get ready to get in two-point when I say."

"What are we going to do?" Amanda asked.

"We're going to jump the wall," Megan explained.

"Oh, no, I couldn't possibly—" Amanda started to protest.

"Want me to leave you in this graveyard?"

"No!" Amanda said fearfully.

"Then you better hold on, and do as I say," Megan said. "It's the only way out of here."

She picked up a trot and pointed Prince at the wall where he'd jumped it before. "Two-point, Amanda!" she yelled as she bent forward and felt

Amanda's grasp around her waist tighten. Prince rocked back on his powerful hindquarters and launched himself effortlessly over the wall.

They both managed to stay on as he landed on the other side. Megan patted his big white neck and turned him toward home. They hadn't gone more than a hundred yards when they heard someone calling.

"Megan! Megan, can you hear me?"

Megan recognized her brother's voice, and then she saw him come through the trees on Popsicle. "Max!" she yelled.

Max wore a worried expression, but when he saw her, he smiled with relief. "There you are. Oh! You found Amanda!" He cantered up to them. "Meg, where have you been? When you didn't show up at the tree, we were worried. Keith and Chloe and I have been all over the pasture looking for you. Then, when Pixie showed up alone, I was afraid you might have fallen off or something. Keith and Chloe just went back to tell Jake and Sharon we couldn't find you." Max shook his head and said, "Man, are we going to be in trouble with Jake and Sharon."

"No, we're not," Megan said. "Not when they see we've found Amanda."

They made their way back to the barn. By the time they got there, the rain had stopped and the sun was beginning to break through the clouds. They put Popsicle and Prince Charming in their stalls and went to the office.

Megan hesitated outside the office door. She saw that Chloe and Keith were sitting on the beat-up old couch, looking uncomfortable. Sharon was dialing the phone. Jake stood with his hands in his hip pockets, frowning at Chloe and Keith. Then Chloe looked up and saw Megan standing outside the office door.

"Megan!" she shrieked.

Jake turned around. Sharon hung up the phone. She stood up at the same time Jake sat down. Megan, Max, and Amanda came into the office.

"Amanda?" Keith said, peering around Sharon.

"Thank goodness," Sharon said, sitting down again.

"Now, where have y'all been?" Jake said, standing up again. "We were just about to call the police! Amanda, what on earth happened to you?"

Megan and Amanda explained what had happened, starting from the campout, when Megan thought she had seen a ghost in the old barn. She explained that Amanda's white gown made her think she was the ghost of the girl who'd died in the fire. Amanda said she must have been sleepwalking when she fell into the trapdoor of the tunnel. Then the wind blew the door shut. Amanda had had no idea where she was in the pitch-black tunnel. She had called out, but no one had heard her over the storm. Then she'd crawled up on an old pile of sacks and fallen asleep. When she woke up, she groped her way down the narrow passage, wading through knee-deep water, until she came to the end of the tunnel. There she could feel fresh air and see a bit of light. Then she waited.

Megan explained how she'd gone looking for Amanda and come upon the old cemetery. She told how she'd found the angel gravestone with the name on it that matched the initials on the locket. Then she told how Prince Charming had helped her three times.

"Well, I'll be," Jake said. "Who'd have thought that stubborn horse would ever have been so useful?"

"There's one thing I don't understand," Sharon said. "How did you know where to find the end of the tunnel?"

"I had a little help from an old friend," Megan admitted. She told them about Marley's journal.

Early in the evening of the next day, when all the barn chores were done and the horses had been fed, Max, Megan, Chloe, and Keith all piled in the back of Jake's pickup truck and went up to the old barn. Jake had brought a ladder. They all climbed up into the loft. Megan went to the window, where she'd left the old journal, but there was nothing there.

"I left it right here," Megan said, searching the floor of the loft for the fifth time. "I know I did!"

She knelt before the little window and looked out over the pastures and hills. Another rainstorm had come that afternoon and left everything dripping and cool. The sun was low and orange in the pale sky.

"I almost wish I really had seen Marley's ghost," Megan said. "If I saw her now, I guess I wouldn't be scared."

"Ghosts aren't real, Megan," Jake said. "Only fear is real. And we only fear the things we don't know about."

"I think I know Marley Dellbrook," Megan said softly. She was peering intently out the window, looking down toward the farthest fence. Suddenly, she put up her hand and waved a little wave.

Only Max saw it. "Who are you waving at?" he asked his sister.

But Megan didn't answer. She closed her hand on the locket that hung around her neck and smiled a small smile, thinking of a girl riding across a ridge at sunset, on a white horse.

About the Author

Allison Estes grew up in Oxford, Mississippi. She wrote, bound, and illustrated her first book when she was five years old, learned to drive her grandfather's truck when she was eight, and got her first pony when she was ten. She has been writing, driving trucks, and riding horses ever since.

Allison is a trainer at Claremont Riding Academy, the only riding stable in New York City. She currently lives in Manhattan with her seven-year-old daughter, Megan, who spends every spare moment around, under, or on horses.

SADDLE UP FOR MORE ADVENTURES WITH MEGAN, MAX, CHLOE, KEITH AND AMANDA IN

SHORT STIRRUP CLUB™ #3
THE GREAT
GYMKHANA GAMBLE
(Coming in mid-July 1996)

What could be more fun than a gymkhana—a day of games on horseback? Of course, it's not always easy to stay on the horse while riding bareback, reaching for flags or weaving around obstacles. But Max hasn't fallen off in years. And he's not about to start now! Megan's furious with her twin when he refuses to enter the contest; now they have to ask Amanda to join their team. Megan vows to prove to her brother that the team can win without him. But when her reckless riding leaves her injured and the team in last place, it's up to Max to overcome his fears and prove that he and Popsicle are really team players.